"We hate to date but we want to get married.

You can't get married unless you go out and find some guy who's willing to pair up with you, so we're all doomed. There's no solution," Ariel said.

"I think I may have a solution," I said.

"Is this solution really complicated?" Frances asked.

"No. It's actually quite simple. We form a group, and we support each other."

"We form a group around dating?" Wendy said, clearly puzzled.

"Yeah," I replied. "We hate to date, right? But we have to date in order to find a guy. So we form a support group, like our book group. Only, instead of discussing depressing works of art, we discuss our dates, our strategies and our plans. We help each other see the flaws in our approaches. We give each other encouragement when we're down."

"And the ultimate goal is?" Ariel said.

"Love."

Elda Minger

Elda Minger is the bestselling, award-winning and versatile author of dozens of romance novels, including series, contemporary and historical. She is also known for her informative and entertaining workshops on writing. The I Hate To Date Club was inspired by all the stories her single girlfriends told her over the years. Elda lives in California with her family, both two- and four-footed, and is currently at work on another novel for Harlequin's NEXT line.

THE I HATE TO DATE CLUB

Elda Minger

THE I HATE TO DATE CLUB

copyright © 2006 Elda Minger

isbn 0373880936

TheNextNovel.com

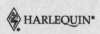 HARLEQUIN®

PRINTED IN U.S.A.

To Judi Hall, my friend since grade school.
If we only knew then what we know now! Some of the
best parts of my childhood were spent with you.

And to Anthony, the apple of your eye.

I hate to date.

I swear it's not just me—burned, hurt, disillusioned too many times to count by now. Take any woman over the age of thirty-five and barely *mention* the prospect of dating. Subtly slip the subject into casual conversation. You'll see a reaction akin to that of a terrified horse galloping out of a burning barn, the whites of its wide eyes showing, total fear in every line of its equine body as it runs for its life.

Or an even sadder reaction, a kind of quiet desperation. A desperate optimism of the "someday my prince will come" variety.

I could go on, but I won't. For now.

No, I will. Just a little longer.

It was different when you were younger. It just was. When you dated in high school or college, everyone and everything you needed was right there, completely set up for you. The machinery that encouraged us to pair off in neat sets of twos was all in place. There were situations, events that made dating easier: dances, football games, clubs, classes, hangouts, lunch hours, that cute boy next door, that excellent bad boy on his motorcycle, the guy in your dorm, your mother's meddling, house parties when your parents were out of town, school trips, the privacy of a dorm room, coed sleepovers—

But I digress. Women of a certain age hate to date. I know this. We all know this, deep inside. But we never really talk about it, we hate it that much.

You'll see what I mean as I get on with my day. Saturday, to be exact. A Saturday in early January, just after the holidays, in sunny Southern California.

I headed toward my van, braving the pouring rain at six-twenty in the morning in the Von's Supermarket parking lot on the corner of Lake and California in Pasadena. Michelle, one of my oldest and dearest friends, was sitting slumped over in the passenger seat inside, unable to face the small crowd inside the Starbucks near the Von's.

She'd called me early this morning sounding emotionally devastated, and asked me to meet her for coffee. Once we'd met in the parking lot, pulling up in adjacent parking spaces, she'd told me she didn't have the strength to go inside and deal with all those happy people getting their morning coffee.

So I had gone inside and gotten us both coffee—two

caramel lattes—and now was running back through the rain to my car. Her sleek black Volvo was parked next to my van.

Michelle was in total meltdown. Her husband left her last night.

Now, it's not like her marriage hadn't been in trouble for a long while. From about the third year, I'd say. Michelle knew this. *I* knew this. We rarely talked about it because I sensed she didn't want to face what was happening. And I wasn't about to bring up that painful subject; I remembered that whole thing about killing the messenger. Life could be depressing enough without discussing it to death.

I knew what it was like to want to live like an Egyptian crocodile, in denial, and I granted my closest friends that same privilege.

Over the years Michelle and her husband, Bryan, grew apart, until they just kind of coexisted. Her life was similar to mine. We were both basically single, except that my two cats and my dog were much better company than her husband. More affectionate and *much* more considerate.

Nevertheless, it was a totally different thing when a man actually left you, even when he really hadn't been there for you for years. When he announced, after three years of cohabiting and eleven years of marriage—that's *fourteen* years of your life!—that he wanted out, wanted a divorce and, worst of all, that he'd fallen in love and had another woman lined up to take your place, well, you stopped dead in your tracks.

That's when you know it's serious. When a man has already scoped out his next significant other, he's already moved on. It's a done deal.

And whether or not you still cared, it sucked big time to be dumped. Because on top of all the turmoil and trouble and emotional pain descending upon your head, you now had to date again.

Michelle knows this. I know this. But I won't say the dreaded D-word. She has enough on her plate. We won't talk about dating, only if she brings it up. But I hope she doesn't. Things were grim enough already today.

Dating. I mean, what kind of a word is that? Dating. Shouldn't we be calling it something else once we're past our thirtieth birthday? Couldn't we introduce something else into the language that didn't sound so—so juvenile?

I opened the driver's-side door, the warmth of the van making up for the cold, damp wetness outside. January in Southern California, and we were having rain like Florida in hurricane season. If it wasn't earthquakes or fires, it was mudslides. Even an older guy on my block who moved to Southern California in the early 1960s says he never saw it pour like this, without end.

A sadly too perfect metaphor for Michelle's meltdown.

I slipped into the driver's seat, silently handed her one of the lattes, then set mine in the closest drink holder.

"Thanks," she said as I closed the door. Michelle, usually a live wire, a real sparkler, my bubbly blond friend who made me laugh harder than anyone, was dead quiet. A bad sign. I stayed silent, picked up my latte, sipped it to give her time.

This was horrible. I hated seeing her in this much pain. She is one of the best people I know and didn't deserve this. But who ever said life was fair?

She blew on her coffee to cool it, then took another small careful sip, as if any movement at all hurt.

"Eva, it's not like I didn't know we had significant problems," she said after a few minutes. Her voice sounded husky. She had clearly been crying for who knew how long, not just a little. Letting out all that emotion she'd been repressing all those years.

"I knew," she said, then took another tiny sip of coffee.

I understood. No woman wanted to look dumb. No one wanted to feel like she didn't see it coming, even if in reality the breakup hit her with the force of a Mack truck. It was always worse when you didn't see it, that horrible cliché of "being the last to know."

I nodded my head. Whatever I thought of Bryan, now wasn't the time to get into it. Michelle needed my support, not my sarcasm, my pithy comments about the war between the sexes. And really, what could I say? It was just a situation that truly sucked.

"She's twenty-two," Michelle whispered. "A year younger than when Bryan and I met. A baby."

I glanced at her, seeing the bewildered anguish in her blue eyes. She was holding in all these new realizations and feelings. It was simply too much to process. She wasn't able to face it yet, and who could blame her? She was thirty-eight, the same as me. We went to high school together. How, in your late thirties, could you compete with a girl just starting her life?

Twenty-two seems like several lifetimes ago.

Forget older and wiser. Most men I observe choose younger and dumber.

"Twenty-two," I said softly, just to let her know I was listening. I didn't know this girl's name, but I'd bet money it's something like Bambi, or Kiki, or Bunny. My girlfriend Ariel called them "the eee-eees."

"I can't...I don't...Eva, what am I going to do?"

I didn't know. I could tell her that she was still young (not compared to Kiki, but...). They had no children, and she'd kept her career going. She was a professional makeup artist who worked regularly on movies.

They'll sell the house they bought together, they'll divide up their finances and pension plans and property and books and DVDs and furniture, their linens and towels, and separate all the cookware. She'll take the photo album and go through that phase where she'll cut his head out of every wedding photo—

It was all so sad.

I tried to look on the bright side—she'll never have to deal with her in-laws again.

"Eva, I'm too old to start over," she said. Defeatedly.

I knew the feeling. And I knew what Michelle really meant.

I cannot do this again. I cannot have my heart broken again. I can't afford to hope again. I cannot open myself up again. I cannot even consider having sex again.

And I sure as hell don't want to date again.

We all know what's out there.

"I know," I said softly, staring out the windshield as the rain poured over the glass, rivulets streaming down like some crazy guy's standing on top of the van and dumping buckets of water on top of us. The side windows were fogged up, but it suited me fine on this Saturday morning. No one could see in, no one could see Michelle's swollen red eyes, her unwashed hair pulled back in a clumsy ponytail. Both her hands shook as she lifted the coffee cup to her chapped lips.

No lipstick, a sure sign of depression. Well, maybe only in my opinion. I collected lipsticks the way Carrie Bradshaw from *Sex and the City* collected Manolos.

I started up the van.

"Do we have to go?" she said. I could feel her panic as she clutched her latte in her hands.

"Nope." I turned on the heater, which was the point of starting the van. Within minutes it was toasty inside, the rain merely noise as it drummed down on the metal roof.

I didn't know what to say. People always say it's enough to just listen, it's more than most people will do. But I was one of those types who needed to fix it. I hated to see people I love hurting.

"You want to stay at my place for a while?" I suggested. I didn't know what was going on, when she was moving out, if she was moving out, if she'd told her family, who would get their vacation home in Big Bear—

"Eva?" she said.

"Yeah?"

Michelle set her coffee down and turned toward me, and I could see the tears running down her cheeks.

"Oh, Eva, I'm going to have to go out there again."

I was silent for a moment.

"Not right away," I said, trying to look on the most minuscule of bright sides. "You'll need some time."

She nodded her head, turned, took hold of her coffee again as if it was a lifeline. I was glad I got her a grande latte with caramel.

"I don't know what to do," she whispered.

"Don't do too much right away," I said, reaching for her hand. *Yeah, right, as if I know what I'm doing.* She held on tightly, as if she was a little girl and I was her mother. "Don't do too much, Micki. And let the people who love you help you, okay?" *And get a really good divorce lawyer…*

"Okay," she whispered, then set her cup down again, pulled her hand away from mine and covered her face with her hands.

"I just don't get it," I said, glancing around the room and keeping my voice low. "Why is it in every single one of these novels, the minute the woman has sex, she's dead soon afterward?"

I was at my monthly book group a few days later, sitting on a couch in Paige Sinclair's spacious living room in San Marino. It had all started innocently enough. A bunch of us had taken a literature class through UCLA Extension in Westwood. I'd enrolled just to get out of my rut. And I've always been self-conscious because I'd dropped out of college during my junior year abroad.

I'd gone to Rome for a year, immediately falling in love with the people, the city and the food. I'd discovered my true passion, signed up for culinary school and became a caterer. Food, prepared with care and love, made people happy. More to the point, I had a chance of making a living doing something I really loved. Why did I have to learn about philosophy when a great alfredo sauce added a lot more happiness to the world?

Anyway, I had taken the literature class to shore up my lack of education and also in the hope of meeting a nice guy who might be able to read and carry on a decent conversation. I'd ended up reading and discussing a few really great books and I'd met some terrific women. The class, though, had been about ninety percent female, with a few gay men thrown in for good measure. The one straight guy had looked young enough to be my teenage son. And I wasn't going there. No attraction, besides.

"You're right," said Ariel, staring down at the trade paperback novel in her hands as if it were a live grenade. "Sex always leads to death. What is it with men that they keep writing this stuff where women keep getting punished for expressing their sexuality?"

I loved Ariel. She was into the most fascinating stuff, and she always took the conversation to a new, and better, level.

"Hey, it's not all men," I replied. "What about that story we read last month, where the woman swam out into the ocean and just drowned after all that happened to her?"

"*The Awakening*," Ariel said. She always remembered names and places and book titles and who really starred in what movie or won which Oscar. I admired the fact that she could keep it all in her head.

"And what about that play at the Pasadena Playhouse we all went to?"

"*Hedda Gabler*. I see what you mean, Eva."

Frances walked into the room. She's been really pro-active in our relationship. She's called me a couple of times and we've gone out to the movies. She's been over to my house; I've been to her place in Silverlake. Over coffee, she'd asked if I'd needed any help with my catering, and I've hired her for a couple of events. I got the feeling Frances was a jill-of-all-trades. Every time I've hired her as a waitress or a bartender, I've been more than pleased with the results. She was fast on her feet, great with people and could take action in a crisis.

She also has a lot of presence and lights up a room when she enters it. You couldn't miss her. She was tall, with spectacular red hair. She'd look right at home in a Titian painting.

We were just finishing up the food break at the end of the meeting and now we had to decide what book to read for next month. Paige had this fetish about the food matching the novel's ambience and atmosphere, so we had Russian going today, blini with sour cream and caviar, borscht, a hearty beef stew and lots of vodka. Okay by me, even though I didn't really care much for caviar. But as a caterer, I know there are people out there who do. I guess I should count myself lucky Paige wasn't serving venison.

Almost a year ago we read a novel called *Smilla's*

Sense of Snow (excellent, by the way), and for one horrible week I was sure Paige was going to come up with a plate of blubber for the break. Or something worse.

"All right, people!" Paige called out, entering the room. She had that rich-family, trust-fund, tall-and-skinny thing going. She was wearing pressed khakis and an emerald-green pullover sweater over a—I swear to God—white blouse with a Peter Pan collar. Of course, a string of pearls and they weren't fake. And leather driving moccasins that I was sure cost the earth. Her hair was perfectly bobbed to her chin, with gorgeous highlights. She had either been on vacation at a beach resort or had an extensive session with a colorist in Beverly Hills.

I'm guessing the colorist at about three to six hundred bucks.

"Okay!" Paige said, sitting down in one of the two leather club chairs across from the sofa where Ariel and I were sitting. Ariel has been my friend since my move to Los Angeles over a decade ago. I'd met her the first week I lived here. We'd just clicked. She was funny and tiny and gorgeous in a Natalie Wood kind of way and worked for a publishing company out in Santa Monica, so she added a lot to our understanding of books. She was also writing a screenplay, but she swore me to total secrecy. So I've never mentioned it to anyone.

I like most of the women in the group. Most of us have been together for almost three years, and I knew I would miss them if we didn't get together once a month.

I genuinely liked Paige, even though her take-charge attitude sometimes got on my nerves. There were times I felt she thought she was better than—no, *superior* to—most women, thanks to her to-the-manner-born attitude. She made a big deal about the fact that she went to a private girls' school back East called Emma Willard, or something like that. "Jane Fonda went there, you know." She'd managed to work that into the first conversation we'd ever had.

And from the outside, I guess Paige really seemed to have the perfect life. An incredibly beautiful home in possibly the wealthiest area of L.A., a good-looking husband, even a golden retriever. No kids yet, but they'd be coming in time and no doubt attending only the best private schools.

But it had been Paige who'd suggested we continue the reading group after the UCLA class had ended. She was a generous person, opening up her home to our group and organizing everything. We all got along well, and we laughed a lot as we got through our various book picks.

The trouble was, I didn't finish reading most of them. It was my dirty little secret.

Leo Tolstoy's *Anna Karenina* sat on my bedside table all through the month of December and the first week of January. Every time I glanced at that book I got a case of the guilts. We'd thought of not reading a book during the holidays, but Paige had convinced all of us that we didn't want to lose momentum. So *Anna Karenina* it was.

I knew Paige's choice had a lot to do with the fact that Oprah had once picked it for her book club. And if it was good enough for Oprah, it was good enough for Paige. She watched Oprah's show religiously, subscribed to her magazine and believed that if Oprah said something, it was the gospel truth.

Hence, *Anna Karenina*.

"Anyone have any suggestions?" Paige said as all of us settled on various sofas, chairs and hassocks. The large living room, furnished with antiques and nineteenth-century oil paintings, resembled a reading room straight out of the Huntington Library. Yikes.

Wendy placed her tea down on the coffee table, careful to use a coaster. "How about something a little lighter?"

"Lighter," said Paige, considering. "In what way?"

"I was thinking, maybe—a romance novel."

Paige's perfect, pert nose wrinkled in disgust, as if a bad smell suddenly had wafted through the room. I knew what was coming. Oprah didn't like romance novels either, so clearly this was not going to go over well with Paige.

"Oh, no. We can't read one of those books."

I couldn't leave Wendy to fight this battle alone. "What, you mean you don't want to read about a woman who might actually have sex and live to tell the tale?"

Everyone laughed. I could always be counted on for a little comic relief, even if I didn't do all the reading.

"What exactly do you mean, Eva?"

I warmed to my subject. "The last three novels we've read, *Madame Bovary*, *The Awakening*, and now *Anna Karenina*, all the women in these stories were punished because they had sex and enjoyed it. They either had sex outside their marriage or they took a lover, or they realized what was missing in their marriage and decided to go looking . . ." I paused and changed the subject in midsentence. "But that's not the point. I think that what Wendy is saying is that she'd like to read a novel where the main character might actually survive the experience."

"Yeah, that sounds like fun," said Frances.

"I don't know," said Paige slowly, and I had to give her credit for not going with a flat-out no. "I just don't see how these novels contribute anything really meaningful. Shouldn't we stick with the classics?"

"We need a break," Wendy said. "Or at least I do. Does anyone else feel this way?"

I raised my hand and glanced around. Ariel's hand was up in the air, along with my own and Frances's. The other four members of the group, including Paige, were not interested.

It was a tie.

"Well," said Paige, picking up her tea and glancing brightly around the living room. "I was thinking about something by Sylvia Plath."

"Isn't she the poet who stuck her head in the oven?" Wendy said, and I groaned.

"Now, Wendy, suicide isn't all she writes about," Paige admonished her gently. She took a deep breath, and I could see that she was making an effort. "What did you have in mind?"

"I read this great novel by Rosamunde Pilcher over the holidays called *Winter Solstice*. The heroine was in her fifties, or maybe even her early sixties, and—"

"That doesn't sound like a romance novel," Paige commented.

"It's a relationship novel, but I really loved it and I would love to discuss it in this group."

"Does she die?" I asked.

"No," said Wendy.

"Punished in any way?"

"Nope," said Wendy.

"Any trains? Loaded guns in dresser drawers? Oceans? Poisons? Is she still even *having* sex at sixty?" I asked.

"Eva!" Paige said.

"Yes," said Wendy. "Yes, she did have sex and I really loved her character." She turned to Paige, making an all-out entreaty. "Please, can we try it, Paige? Just this once? Just something a little different for February."

"For Valentine's Day," I said, and watched Paige carefully. She was softening. Maybe there was some romance in her soul after all.

"Oh, I—all right. What was the title? *Winter Solstice?*"

"Yes," said Wendy, settling back on the sofa and picking up her tea, relieved that she'd won this round.

"Is it in paperback?"

"Yes. She's a popular author, she's been on the *New York Times* bestseller list several times at least. I'm sure any Borders or Barnes & Noble carries it. And there's always Amazon."

I noticed that Paige recoiled slightly from the word *popular*, as if any novel that's popular was slightly tainted. And I wondered, not for the first time, why an author would want to be *unpopular*. Wasn't the whole point of writing to reach people with your work?

But at least Wendy won this time. Maybe later down

the road we could sneak in some Dean Koontz or Michael Crichton. Now, they were authors whose books I wouldn't mind seeing on my bedside table. I might even read them.

"Then it's all settled." Paige glanced around the living room, then said, "I'll e-mail all of you with the title information, and a reminder of the meeting date in February."

Now we could just talk and enjoy ourselves.

I need to make one thing clear. Since I didn't usually make it through the whole book, I didn't just coast along, letting all the other women in the group—and Phil, our one gay guy—do all the work. I didn't just come here, make jokes and stuff myself. No, I prepared for this day like an Olympic athlete. I rented the movie, if available, and seriously skimmed the Cliff's Notes. Sometimes the movie veered off in unusual directions, so the Cliff's Notes were a backup. But I had a feeling I'd be finishing—and enjoying—*Winter Solstice*.

"Nice work," I said, whispering to Wendy.

She smiled, then set down her tea. "Eva, would you meet me at the Starbucks on Lake and California after the meeting? I've asked Frances along as well."

I wasn't sure what this was about, but I liked Wendy a lot. I didn't socialize with her, but we talked on the phone quite a bit and I enjoyed seeing her at our group.

"Sure. Ariel was going to come over to my place after the meeting, so do you mind if she comes along, too?"

"Not at all. I'd like her input."

"This sounds serious."

"It is." She hesitated. "I'm just confused and I need some good advice."

And she's asking me? I once had a therapist who advised me, "Now, Eva, you simply cannot make judgments by looking at other people's exteriors. You don't know what they're going through."

True enough. But in this case, my exterior must be doing really well, because it had no bearing on how my life sometimes resembled a complete train wreck. (No pun intended, considering our last literary selection.)

I wished I was more organized. I wished I planned for the future better, especially financially. I wished I had a clue as to what I was doing on this planet, other than racing through each day, barely able to cram all the stuff I had to do into each moment.

Don't get me wrong. I cooked quite a few good meals along the way, and I loved making people happy. Caterers were present at most of the great milestones of life, at birthdays and weddings, graduations and christenings, at really happy occasions. There were also anniversary dinners, and more and more events over the holidays like Thanksgivings and Christmases.

Women were getting smarter and realizing that they didn't *have* to do anything—or everything. Being a superwoman was so over. For the right price, they could pick up the phone and order in, or order *me* to come in and cook for them.

There were also the funerals and the other get-togethers that weren't that cheery. (Many a family reunion I've catered was right up there.) I also made sure to fix several meals a month for AIDS patients, and I had a list of elderly people that I cooked for, so I did try to balance it all out.

But I didn't consider my life to be truly balanced at all. Wendy thought I was a good person to ask for advice? I hated to destroy her illusions, so I tried to do my best and call it a day.

CHAPTER 2

We were in line at Starbucks after our book group and I still had no idea what Wendy wanted to talk about. I probably knew her the least of all four of us, as she's been in the book group less than a year. I know Ariel the best—we've been friends for years. And Frances and I get along well.

Wendy intimidated me at first, quite possibly because she truly was a spectacular-looking woman. I have a couple of women friends who are always telling me how beautiful they were, and how much trouble their lives were because of all that beauty. In my book, if you had to keep making a point of how gorgeous you were, you weren't that secure about your looks. And you probably weren't all that beautiful.

I had a specific criterion about looks. To be considered gorgeous, I had to see someone of the opposite sex literally walk off the sidewalk, into a signpost, into a parked car when he caught sight of you, just like in a cartoon or a slapstick-movie scene.

I have known of women who have caused traffic collisions while walking down the street. Now, *that* was power.

I have only ever seen that happen with Wendy.

If a casting director were sizing me up, I'd land the part of "the heroine's best friend." Not so much Rosie O'Donnell or Joan Cusack, but more like Meg Ryan during her romantic-comedy heyday. The proverbial girl next door. I have made my peace with it.

The four of us—me, Ariel, Frances and Wendy—all went out for coffee once after our book group. I watched a man who—after doctoring his coffee—had seen Wendy and walked straight into one of the walls, spilling his coffee all over the front of his Brooks Brothers shirt in the process. Luckily he hadn't careened into one of the displays, with all the breakable mugs, glass coffeepots and other coffee paraphernalia.

Don't talk to me about gorgeous. I know gorgeous and gorgeous is Wendy. She had that Snow White coloring, black hair, blue eyes, and flawless pale skin that literally took your breath away. Lips as red as a red, red rose and all that. You get the picture. It was the same kind of beauty that Elizabeth Taylor had when she was young. Or Ava Gardner. Charlize Theron. Breathlessly stunning good looks.

So now we were all standing in line for coffee, and I hadn't a clue what was going on. I wasn't even all that flattered that Wendy thought my life was in such great shape that she was going to ask me for advice. Something happened today at the book group, and I thought it had something to do with the fact that I'd stood up for Wendy and her request for a different sort of book.

I might have done it in my usual humorous way, not taking things too seriously, but I hadn't left her hanging out to dry. I'd stuck with her, and for some reason that had counted for something with Wendy.

I also had the kind of face, or presence, or demeanor, or whatever it was, that led people to open up to me, and I mean *really* open up to me. The stories I've *heard* from people during catering gigs—unbelievable. Marriages on the rocks, children with drug problems, in-laws that are driving a person to suicidal thoughts. One guy was a cross-dresser.

About the only thing I haven't heard was a murder confession. I listen to it all, while making another pot of good strong coffee and scrounging around among all the leftover food for something that resembled a little snack (you had to keep the blood sugar up, for both the confessor and the confessee). I quietly packed up the food and cleaned up, then sat down at various kitchen tables in the houses of the rich and sometimes famous and I just listened.

I'm originally from Illinois. I came from a long

heritage of being able to solve anything over a pot of coffee—Swedish plasma, as my mom used to call it—and a plate of brownies. (From scratch, of course.)

And I kept all their secrets. I wouldn't stay in business very long if I hadn't.

Wendy was ahead of me, ordering her coffee, and she looked nervous. Frances was right behind her, then me, and then Ariel.

Ariel was scoping the place out. For someone who was so petite—she was barely five foot two—she always knew what was going on.

"Those couches in the far corner are clearing up," she said now. "I'll go stake a claim if you'll get me my usual."

"A decaf triple grande cinnamon no-whip mocha, right?"

"You got it." She hitched her shoulder bag a little higher on her petite frame and headed over to the corner and the comfy sofas.

Within about fifteen minutes, we were all sitting around Wendy, coffees and treats in hand, waiting to hear what this was all about.

"I want to thank you guys for coming," Wendy said softly, glancing around the coffeehouse to make sure no one was paying any attention to us. But that was impossible, because there were a few men in the place, and they'd already zeroed in on Wendy.

She lowered her voice and leaned in closer.

"I just moved here from New York almost six months ago. I was doing some modeling—"

It was no stretch to imagine Wendy as a model. And this was true—she has only been in the book group for a few months. Just enough time to have gotten a nice dose of death by poisoning, drowning and throwing oneself beneath a speeding train.

"—but I wanted to make a brand-new start for myself when I came to Los Angeles."

Okay, so far so good.

"But something happened this morning that caught me completely off guard."

I took a sip of my coffee, listening.

"I'm kind of ashamed to admit this—" She falters, and Frances reached over and put a reassuring hand on her shoulder.

"You can tell this group anything," she said confidently. "We're good people here."

I glanced at both her and Ariel. And me. Yes, we were. Solid, no-nonsense women.

Wendy stared at the table for a long moment, then took a deep breath and said ever so quietly, "I want to get married."

I had just finished swallowing some of my coffee, and thank God for that, because if I'd been in mid-swallow it might have come right back out my nose. Wendy, gorgeous Wendy, was having trouble finding a man? This made no sense. The world has gone mad.

It was like back when Brad Pitt and Jennifer Aniston announced their separation and all of Hollywood—hell, the world—had reeled in shock. And then they'd divorced. And if these two gorgeous people couldn't make a marriage work with their fantastic looks, their spectacular success and tons of money, what hope was there for us mere mortals?

I knew this was a very shallow attitude. But I was working on it. I knew that movie stars had the same problems with intimacy that normal people did, perhaps even more because of the nature of their business. But you had to admit, it didn't make any sense that a woman as stunning as Wendy should have trouble finding a man.

My intuition was screaming at me that there was more to this story than she was telling us. But I also had the feeling that she was going to tell us the rest of it, and soon. Patience, patience…

"Do you have a boyfriend now?" asked Ariel. "Is it serious?" Trust her to start getting the facts down so we could solve the problem. Ariel was the friend I called at four o'clock in the morning whenever I was having a problem. She got the facts from you, sorted them out and convinced you that things weren't as bad as they seemed. She was like one of those women in a forties movie, a woman's movie, so smart and empowered. Rosalind Russell. Myrna Loy.

"Sort of."

Uh-oh. This didn't sound good. I imagined something—someone—locked in a deep, dark cellar, then shook my head just the tiniest bit to clear the image from my overactive imagination. I was having visions straight out of *Rebecca*, but that was an attic, wasn't it? Or was that *Jane Eyre?* Ariel would know. I could never keep it all straight.

"What does that mean, 'sort of'?" Ariel asked gently. She was so terrific at pulling information out of people before they even realized what it was they were revealing.

"He's—it's complicated."

He's married. I know it. I could feel it. Or involved with someone else, or engaged to someone else, or gay, or about to be married this weekend, or married to her sister, or—oh God, I've heard this same story a dozen times before, and I always wondered about the women who told me about these guys.

What was it they just didn't get? Like Dr. Phil always said on his show, "If he'll do it with you, he'll do it to you." That, and the old, "Even a pancake has two sides."

My friend Michelle, whose husband recently walked out on her, is a professional makeup artist who worked regularly on movies. Big expensive movies, feature films, with big movie stars. A lot of them came on to her, ignoring her wedding ring.

She's never, ever gone there, no matter how good looking the actor, even if she's had fantasies about him. And boy, has she been tempted. Nothing like being close enough to a stunning man, practically straddling him, to carefully apply his makeup. Touching him. So close and yet so far.

If he'll do it with you, he'll do it to you.

Oh no. Wendy didn't have to throw herself beneath a train, like poor Anna Karenina. She was already there.

The conversation faltered. Wendy was still looking down at the coffee table, and I felt sorry for her. This couldn't be easy. But Frances's hand remained on her shoulder, and Ariel was right across from her. I leaned in and heard Ariel say, "He's not married, is he?"

Wendy nodded her head, that lush black hair of hers catching the low evening light in the coffeehouse.

I kept still, even though part of me wanted to lean back, wanted to say something, wanted to reach across and grab her and shake her and say, "What were you *thinking?*"

Instead, I waited. And thought, *Here we go again.*

CHAPTER 3

I've always gone with my gut, and it's served me well. Whenever I haven't, I've regretted it. And my gut was telling me that we all needed to help Wendy. She was in a lot of agony over this married guy, and she needed support. Far be it from me to judge. She'd decided to confide in the three of us, which told me she hadn't made too many other friends in the months she'd been in Los Angeles.

L.A. can be a tough city when it comes to making friends. I have a lot of acquaintances, but few true friends. It's such a career-oriented town, and pretty competitive. The best of the best come here to get work, get successful fast, and there's no place at the table for slackers.

I moved here with Michelle over a decade ago, and I couldn't have done without her. I had Michelle, and then I met Ariel early on, so I'd had two excellent friends right from the start. I sensed Wendy hadn't had such good luck. I could see how looks like hers could be off-putting to a certain type of female friend, the type who was into competition and who believed in a scarcity of resources.

So my gut made up my mind, as usual. I was in.

I shifted forward even more, almost falling onto the large coffee table.

"What happened this morning?" I asked.

Wendy glanced up, looking blankly at me for a moment. I could tell she was just not processing, probably because she was deeply ashamed of admitting she was involved with someone who was married. It took a lot for her to come clean with it. You didn't fantasize about your future as a young girl and say, "I want to get involved in a hopeless relationship with a married man!" This was not what you were dreaming as you dressed up with your mother's lace tablecloth on your head and played at getting married. Not that I ever did that...

"What happened this morning that made you want to get married?" I asked, then sat back on the couch a little and waited.

It wasn't long in coming.

"I got a call this morning...from my sister. My little sister. She just got engaged and they're getting married this fall. She was...so *happy*. Ecstatic. She wanted to let me know so I could arrange my schedule, take some vacation time and fly back home for the wedding."

"And that got you thinking about marriage," said Frances. "And family."

Family. The only family a married man got you involved with was his own, because they were usually the reason he was never available.

"Yeah." Wendy smiled, but her expression was tinged with sadness. "And right at that moment, I realized how much *I* wanted to get married. How much I wanted to share my life with a man. When she told me she was getting married I was all upset inside, but I couldn't let her see that. I congratulated her and we talked for a while, but once I hung up the phone all this emotion came up out of me and I couldn't stop crying."

Those beautiful blue eyes were welling up now.

Wendy glanced around at all of us, then said, "I felt like my heart was breaking."

I didn't know what to say. I was absolutely floored by her vulnerability, her honesty. But the rational part of me wanted to tell her that statistics don't lie. They were cold, logical, truthful—and sometimes very painful to hear. Getting involved with a married man was not a good thing.

Only about five percent of marriages that started with infidelity—where one or the other of the couple cheated on their marital partner to create the new relationship—even lasted. *Five percent.* Those were horrible odds.

I usually pushed the whole man-relationship-marriage question to the back of my head. In my early thirties, I'd said to myself, "Eva, you're so young, you don't need to worry about that right now." Thirty-five kind of crept up on me. Thirty-eight slammed me in the face. Forty was right around the corner, and the pickings, as they say, were getting pretty slim.

"I can understand that, Wendy," I replied. "I'd like to get married myself."

I gave Ariel a lot of credit for not laughing out loud. She must have caught the seriousness of the whole thing. I mean, if we were all laying our cards out on the table, why let Wendy go there alone?

"I don't know if I have the courage a relationship needs," Frances said. "I was divorced almost two years ago, and I still feel like I'm getting over it."

"My friend Michelle's husband just walked out on her," I added. "For a twenty-two-year-old."

"I'm dating two guys, and I can't see myself ending up with either of them," Ariel said.

This was getting interesting, like a huge game of truth or dare. I glanced at the other three women and realized that, even if things were just getting good, we wouldn't be able to sustain ourselves on just coffee and bakery treats. Starbucks served sandwiches, but I was thinking of more substantial fare.

"I have an idea." Three pairs of eyes focused on me and, confident that I was doing the right thing, I continued. "I just catered a big Italian family reunion, and I have a fridge full of leftover lasagna, sausage and ziti, and salad. It seems that some of this big Italian family didn't really want to make the party. So how about we all go back to my house and we can sit around, have dinner and continue this?"

No one said no. I wrote out some hurried directions for Wendy on a Starbucks napkin.

As I pulled out of the parking lot and on to California Boulevard, I ran through what I was coming home to in my head. In a burst of incredible luck, I'd vacuumed this morning, and all the dishes were done. I'd even cleaned the cat's litter box. I wasn't a slob, but I would never win any awards for my housekeeping. And I never made my bed. As my little brother used to say to my mother, what was the point?

But if I got there first, and shoved a pan of lasagna into the oven, made garlic bread with real garlic and tossed up what was left of the salad with a killer vinaigrette, who would care?

It's next to impossible to own a home in Southern California. Prices are ridiculously high. When I first moved out here with Michelle, we shared a studio apartment and kept expenses to a minimum. Then she met Bryan and moved in with him. After that, it seemed like I lived in one apartment after another, each one smaller than the next.

Then my great-aunt died. Back home, I used to ride my bike over to see her just because I liked her. As time went on and she got older, I found myself going to see her with an eye toward helping her. I took her shopping, helped her throw food out of her fridge when it got too old, did heavy stuff like vacuuming and yard work.

When I had come home from Italy and my dad was totally pissed at me for dropping out of college and deciding to become a chef, she'd been the one who'd calmed him down. I mean, she had memories of my dad in diapers, so she could do that. She had totally believed in me and in my dream, and that had meant a lot to me. She had even loaned me the money for culinary school, and I'd paid her back, every cent.

She'd left me her house and all her savings.

My dad had helped me sell the house in Illinois and with the money from the sale, I'd managed to buy a small house in South Pasadena. I'd squeaked in right before prices really started to climb. When I'd purchased my home, it was charmingly referred to in the real-estate business as "a real fixer-upper, but with *such* potential!" One roof, new plumbing and electric, some retrofitting and several coats of both indoor and outdoor paint later, along with totally refinished wood floors, and I had been good to go.

I loved it. It was small, a craftsman cottage and a huge front porch with a swing and one of those fireplaces built out of river rock. The street was lined with older trees, so there was plenty of shade. Kids played in the neighbors' yards; I could hear them calling out to each other in the morning during the summer.

I had developed a love of gardening from working in my great-aunt's yard, so I did all my own landscaping. And of course, because this was Pasadena, I planted some roses.

But there were many years when I'd been really house poor, and slept on a mattress on the floor of my bedroom. I had a laundry basket for a dresser. I'd managed with a used sofa and a table and chairs I'd bought from Goodwill. I had been working a regular job, secretarial, a nine-to-five deal, and the catering business had been still a dream. I hadn't even worked my first restaurant job.

But I'd taken it step by step, and now as I opened the front door and walked into my living room, I was satisfied with what I saw.

I ran into the kitchen and put the lasagna into the oven. The weather was still gray and unseasonably cold even for this time of year. It hadn't rained for the Rose Parade, but it had been pouring ever since. I wasn't used to damp cold and cloudy gray skies. That's part of the reason I left my small town in Illinois, to get away from bad weather. It makes me cranky.

So I got a fire going in the fireplace, made sure the pillows on both sofas were plumped up, lit a few candles on the large coffee table, and went back to the kitchen for a bottle of wine.

Ariel arrived first. She's not only tiny, she has a lead foot.

"Play bartender," I said, indicating a bottle of white wine and four glasses. She nodded and headed out toward the living room with all of it, after pouring me a glass. I started on the garlic bread and the vinaigrette.

Single women eating alone. I could do an entire cookbook about it. Sometimes it was just nice to eat with other people.

I hadn't mentioned my cats and I hoped Wendy wasn't allergic. One had come with the house. Bongo was an incredibly fluffy tabby cat. The vet had guestimated his age at around eight, so he was the old man of the house. He'd lived out in the yard for about a week after I'd moved in before he'd figured out I wasn't going to have a hissy fit if he came indoors. Now I couldn't get him to leave if I tried. I'd gotten a kitten to keep him company when I first moved in, and Riley, an orange-and-white blur of incredibly determined and friendly fur, kept things interesting.

My dog, Ming, was a black Pekingese, courtesy of my client's mother, who moved into a nearby retirement home. Anna wasn't allowed to keep him, and was frantic until I'd volunteered to take him in. I'd wanted to get a dog from the moment I'd bought the house. She came to see him a couple of times a month. I baked her favorite cookies and made these visits like a party. I'll never understand why her daughter didn't take Ming in, but I guess you're either a dog person or you aren't.

I could hear the front door opening and Ming barking his red alert. The garlic bread was ready, sliced and spread with butter, minced garlic and seasonings. I was whisking the vinaigrette when Frances walked in.

"Need any help?" She had a glass of white wine in her hand, courtesy of Ariel.

"Nope. Almost done."

"That was nice, what you did for Wendy at the group. What you did for all of us. Jesus, I could use a lift from all those depressing endings. I guess it just doesn't count in fiction unless somebody dies or everybody's left unhappy."

"Good point."

We headed out toward the living room just as Wendy walked up on the porch and tentatively rang the bell.

Ming barked again, once, then twice, sharp little yaps. He looked back at me anxiously as if to say, *I'm doing a good job, aren't I?* He was a little bit neurotic, but given his background, who could blame him? We all dealt with loss in different ways.

I went for the front door to greet Wendy. She'd just made a huge leap in our collective friendship, confiding in all of us about some of her deepest feelings. I didn't want to let her have time to think about what she'd done, or regret it. I wanted to get a glass of wine into her hands as soon as possible.

It was one of those evenings you look back on with such fondness. Absolutely perfect. Good food, good people, great conversation. One of those evenings you just don't want to end. And as it was Saturday night and no one had to go to work the next day, everyone stayed late.

We'd torn through the lasagna and the baked ziti like Garfield on amphetamines, along with the salad and garlic bread. After the first bottle of wine I'd opened a second, but we were slowing down.

I didn't have any dessert on hand, but there was a caterer's trick I'd learned early on in my career. I always had the makings of an excellent cup of coffee in my kitchen. I ground the beans fresh, bought organic coffee and used a French-press coffeepot. I kept a good supply of half-and-half, and I also kept various liqueurs on hand. It made a difference.

I also kept several boxes of truly decadent chocolates in my cupboard. If you put them out on a pretty dessert plate and served them with really great coffee, no one was going to complain.

No one complained tonight. Women and chocolate, what a winning combination.

"This was spectacular, Eva," Wendy said, stretching back on the sofa, Ming snuggled on her lap and looking up at her adoringly after a particularly prolonged tummy rub. "I can't remember when I've enjoyed a dinner more."

"Sure beats eating a sandwich standing over my sink," Ariel said, and Wendy laughed.

"Or cold Chinese out of the carton," Frances said.

"Or a bowl of cereal," I added.

"Okay," said Ariel, and I leaned back in one of the chairs, enjoying the warmth from the fire, knowing that my friend was going to take the conversation in an entirely different direction. Ariel was the one you always wanted at your dinner party. She ensured the conversation would be a smashing success.

"If we're all such great women—and we are—why aren't any of us married? Huh?" She looked around the room, then reached for another chocolate.

Frances and Wendy seemed stumped. But I thought I had the answer.

"It's because," I said, "we all hate to date."

CHAPTER 4

"Hate to date?" Wendy said. "What do you mean?"

"Exactly what I just said. It's horrible, dating. Think about it. When did you last go out with a man on a real date and have a great time? I mean, one of the best nights of your life?"

Silence as all three women thought about this. Silence. And more silence. Which said it all.

"You're not counting something we saw in a movie," Ariel said.

"Or heard about from a friend," said Frances.

"Nope. It had to happen to you. You had to be there on a date."

More silence.

"Maybe you're right and it's not such a great system," Frances said.

"How did they do it in earlier times?" Ariel asked. "If you think about it, dating is a pretty new invention. It just started in the last century. Marriages used to be arranged, didn't they?"

"In some parts of the world they still are," said Wendy.

"And," I added, "arranged marriages are known to have a much higher success rate. The current divorce rate in this country is over fifty percent. Those are crappy odds. But in China and India, they even do horoscopes to ensure that the marriages they arrange will last."

"But," said Ariel, "aren't those marriages really about property and children? Maintaining a family? What about love?"

"What about love?" I countered. "You could say that the current mess we're in is all Hollywood's fault. And the whole love thing. Maybe we expect too much from marriage. Maybe we're too picky and that's why we're all still single."

Everyone mulled this over in silence and I wondered if I'd pushed things too far. That's one of my more endearing qualities. I had a tendency to open my mouth and push my foot right in. Shy with my opinions I wasn't.

"Maybe we do expect too much," Wendy said slowly, and I could tell she was thinking as she spoke. "But maybe we expect too little, especially from our men."

"Amen to that," muttered Frances.

"It's true," Ariel said. "I can remember stories my mom used to tell me about when she and her sisters used to date. Guys would hold doors open, take them out to dinner. Sex wasn't even an issue until they'd get *engaged*. Now if you don't put out by the third date, he doesn't call back."

"Hey, let's not go back to the Dark Ages," Frances said. "A lot of women married their one and only and he was a dud in bed. Can everyone say faking orgasms?"

"Or not even realizing they exist?" said Ariel. "I, for one, am very thankful for the sexual revolution. But sometimes I wish we could get a little of that old stuff back. Some of the magic."

"But some things remain the same," I argued. "I was at the bookstore the other day and you wouldn't *believe* the pile of books on relationships! They have their displays all set up for Valentine's Day, but it seems like the more we learn about people and relationships, the more complicated it gets."

Frances was about to add something to the conversation when there was a sudden, sharp knock at the front door. Ming barked but remained in Wendy's lap. I got up out of my chair and went toward the door, then peered through the peephole.

Michelle. And she didn't look good.

I opened the door and she sort of fell inside. I noticed the two large suitcases and her makeup case on the front porch with her.

"Eva, I'm so sorry, I should have called—"

"No, no, don't be—"

She stepped inside, then suddenly became aware that we weren't alone.

"Oh my God, you have company! I'm so sorry—"

"No, no, in fact, we were all just talking about men and dating." At the look of absolute horror on her face, I quickly changed gears. "I have some lasagna. And ziti. And chocolate."

Michelle looked down at the floor, and I could tell she wished she could just fall through it.

"Come on, you have to be hungry."

"Yeah," she whispered. "I'm not eating too well these days."

"Wine?" Frances said, appearing at her side. "I'm Frances, by the way. Let me get your jacket."

I whipped up another meal at lightning speed. After Michelle had been convinced that she hadn't ruined some sort of party, she went over and sat on the floor by the fire, her plate on the coffee table, and ate her dinner.

"Just go on talking and pretend I'm not here," she said. "I have nothing to add to this conversation. My husband just dumped me for a twenty-two-year-old, so I'm not planning on dating for the rest of this year. Maybe the rest of my life. The thought of it makes me nauseous."

"See?" I said, turning toward the group. "We *hate* to *date*. It's not a natural process. If you grew up on a farm early in the last century, there were a few men in town or on other farms to choose from. Your mother and father probably had someone all picked out, and you met him during those planting times or when you were canning stuff or barn burning—"

"Barn *building*, Eva. Like in *Witness*." Ariel's dark eyes were alive with mischief.

"That's what I meant! And where's Harrison Ford when you need him?"

"The last time I checked," Wendy said, "he was with a much younger woman."

"That's the way it is in the movies," Michelle said around a mouthful of lasagna. "Remember that movie with Sean Connery and Michelle Pfieffer? The one in Russia? She was in her thirties and he was in his sixties."

"Yeah, but you're talking about Sean Connery," Frances said. "James Bond. Be still my heart. That *voice*."

"Point taken," Michelle said, and resumed eating.

"Okay," Wendy said. "We hate to date. It's not a very natural process, and a lot of the basic rules, even manners, have fallen by the wayside. Men expect sex by the third date. There are many who won't even go out with a woman unless she's a lot younger than they are or a model."

"Hey, you're halfway there," Ariel joked.

"Yeah, but I'm thirty-four, so by these standards, I should be looking for a man in his sixties."

"Terrific," Frances muttered. "What about the rest of us, pushing forty?"

"There's always the retirement homes," I suggested. "Just make sure you enjoy playing bingo."

"Come on, Eva," said Frances. "You don't really think a relationship like that could work, do you?"

"Depends."

Everyone groaned and I couldn't blame them, but Frances had set me up with such a great straight line.

"What started this whole conversation?" Michelle asked, pushing her now-empty plate away. I was glad to see she was eating.

"Wendy wants to get married," I said. "We all do."

"It's not what it's cracked up to be, trust me," Michelle replied.

"How long were you married?" Frances asked.

"Fourteen years."

"So you were a pretty young bride."

"Twenty-four and criminally stupid."

I remembered things differently. Michelle had been a beautiful bride, and I'd thought she and Bryan made a great couple. Goes to show how much I know.

"What happened?" Frances asked. "If you don't mind talking about it."

"I don't know." Michelle sighed, then looked into the fire. She was silent for a moment, then said, "No. Maybe I do. I'm just so discouraged and hurt and angry and fucked up. I don't think I can talk about it right now."

"Then don't," Frances said. "I shouldn't have asked."

"It's okay."

"Then there's no solution," Ariel said. "We hate to date but we want to get married. You can't get married unless you go out and find some guy who's willing to pair up with you, so we're all doomed. Our lives are as good as over. We're just waiting for death."

"If you wrote this in a book," Wendy said, "it would be a literary masterpiece. Paige would love it."

"As long as one of us died at the end," Ariel added.

Everyone laughed, even Michelle.

"I think I may have a solution," I said. "More coffee, anyone? I can make another pot."

"Sure. But is this solution really complicated?" Frances asked.

"There aren't any speeding trains involved, are there?" said Ariel.

"No. It's actually quite simple. We form a support group. It's one of women's greatest strengths, the ability to work together."

"We form a group around dating?" Wendy said, clearly still puzzled.

"Yeah," I replied. "We hate to date, right? But we have to date in order to find a guy. Instead of discussing depressing works of fiction like we do in our book group, we would discuss our dates, our strategies and plans. We'll help each other see the flaws in our approaches, give each other encouragement when we're down."

"And the ultimate goal is?" Ariel said.

"Love."

Silence. Then Wendy said, "Isn't that a little optimistic, given what we've just been talking about for the past hour?"

"It is. But I'm going to tell you something my mother once told me. Actually, she told my older sister after this big breakup she had with her boyfriend during her senior year. Meg was devastated, she was sobbing at the kitchen table. My mom let her talk it all out, and when Meg finally asked her what she should do, she said something that I've never forgotten."

"Where were you when all this was going on?" Michelle asked.

"Sitting on the stairs and eavesdropping. Anyway, what she said was this. 'Meg, life can change in a heartbeat. For both good and bad.'"

"That was it?" Ariel said.

"Yes, but don't you get it? At any moment in time, life could change for any one of us. But we have to be out there to meet it. And it's hard. I'm tired at the end of a workweek. I want nothing more than to curl up in bed with a thriller, or watch a DVD, or just take a nap. But none of this is going to get me any closer to finding the right guy. Life doesn't come with any guarantees. You have to go out and meet it head-on, and make your way."

"You've got a point," Frances said. Then, "I'm in. What's this going to involve?"

"I was watching this talk show about dating in the new century," I said, warming to my subject. "The host said there were two things that women had to do. One was to accept every single social invitation you're invited to, even the ones that seem like they could be real disasters. Because you never know who may show up, or who you could meet there."

"What was the second one?" Wendy said. She looked intrigued.

"The second one," I said, "was that you had to go out on one date a week. Period."

Groans and shrieks met this second piece of advice.

"Yep, I know. Hate to date. Sorry, but we have to do it. You have to get out on the field and into the game."

"Eva, you don't even like sports," Ariel pointed out.

"It seemed like a good metaphor at the time." I glanced around my comfortable living room. Wendy,

Ming and Frances were settled on one sofa. Michelle was on the floor in front of the fireplace, Bongo curled up in her lap and purring as she scratched him beneath his furry chin. Ariel was sprawled on the other sofa, with Riley stretched out and snoozing along the back. "All I know is that I don't want to hit forty and look back and realize that I wasn't giving it my best shot."

"You're right," Frances said. "Yep, I'm so in."

"Me, too," Ariel said. "I'm going to give both of my current guys the heave-ho next week!"

The three of us turned to Wendy. Her bottom lip trembled and she bit down on it to stop it, then said, "Would you guys help me get him out of my life? I think I'm going to need some emotional support."

"Count on it," Frances said.

"We'll cover your back," Ariel said.

"Whatever you do," Michelle said as she scratched Bongo behind the ears, his eyes slits of pure ecstasy, "don't marry him if he's a jerk."

No chance of that happening…

"Okay then," I said, picking up my almost empty mug of coffee and raising it high. Everyone joined in, even Michelle. "Here's to the first official meeting of the I Hate to Date Club!"

CHAPTER 5

We were so full of energy that night, so optimistic. It was as if no one in the history of womankind had ever thought up a solution like this. The five of us talked far into the evening, I made another pot of coffee and brought out more chocolate, and our strategy was set up.

The sports metaphors weren't working for everyone, so we decided to go with war. What would an experienced general do before going into battle with his troops? He'd check all the variables; the weather, the terrain, his troops, their supplies, what he knew about the enemy they were about to face. He'd count on his troop's training, know their strengths and weaknesses inside and out. He'd probably even check out the alignment of the planets and the stars.

We'd agreed to meet on alternate Sundays, at my house. Everyone wanted me to provide the food, and they'd all chip in for expenses. To my surprise, we voted to start tomorrow, the very next Sunday. They didn't want this Saturday to count as the first meeting. It was fine by me, as I didn't have a catering job. And I'd already decided to forgo any Sunday lunches for a while. I had to get my personal life in order. I didn't want to be in my eighties and making endless quiches, salads and tarts without a man in sight. The prospect was too damn depressing.

But everyone had assured me that if a catering job came along that I didn't want to pass up, we could meet in the evenings.

"We'll work around everyone's schedules," said Ariel. "And after all, once we get rolling on this whole thing, the meetings should go smoothly."

We were all heartened that the four of us wanted to meet again so soon.

"Today should count as the day we decided to form the club," Ariel said, reaching for just one more chocolate. Like she had to worry. Ever since I've known her she's eaten like a trucker and has had the metabolism of a fifteen-year-old boy athlete. She never put on an ounce. If anything, she had to eat a lot to maintain her weight.

"I agree," said Frances. "What's on the agenda for tomorrow's meeting?"

Wendy didn't say much of anything, and I knew she was thinking about her married boyfriend. Of the four of us, she was the one who probably had the most work to do right from the start. I could tell, from the way she talked about him, that she had a major emotional and sexual attachment to this rat, and it wasn't going to be easy getting him out of her life. But the club could help. I had faith in the power of more than one.

As for Michelle, she was intrigued by this whole thing, but was still raw and bleeding from what her husband had done to her. She would give us what support she could, but the idea of dating was not even on her radar screen.

"Maximize potential," she mumbled around a mouthful of chocolate.

"What?" said Ariel.

"You should all come here tomorrow and each of you should think about your biggest assets and your biggest stumbling blocks to this whole thing," Michelle said. "And I'll help out by giving each of you a mini makeover. I can do eyebrows if anyone wants, because you can change your whole look by what you do with your eyebrows. I can also recommend specific cosmetics that can really bring out your best features." Then she turned to Wendy and said, "You've pretty much got it all going, and I'm assuming that's because you're a model?"

Wendy nodded. "But I'll work on that list. And I'll help you with the makeovers."

"Great!" Frances said. "I've been wanting to try a different look, I'm bored with the same old me. Can we do hair and everything?"

"Absolutely," said Michelle.

"There's a Rite Aid just down the street," I offered. "We could take a break during the meeting and do a little shopping. Colorado Boulevard has a Sephora if the brands Michelle recommends aren't at the drugstore. We could do a recon mission."

Everyone laughed at the war metaphor, even if it was stretching things a bit.

"Perfect!" said Ariel. "I can already tell you one of my problems. I'm always with a bunch of men, so I'm either seen as their little sister or one of the guys. I'd like to change that dynamic."

"Easy peasy," said Michelle. "It's all in the attitude, but a lot can be helped along with makeup, hair and clothes."

"I can help with clothes," offered Wendy. "I've picked up a lot of hints over the years, all the modeling jobs. Being around the stylists really helped me with my own wardrobe."

"I can help with color," said Frances. When everyone looked at her, she shrugged and said, "I paint landscapes in my spare time. I think I have a pretty good eye for color. On other people anyway."

"I," said Ariel, "will bring a pile of dating and self-help books that I've read and offer a mini report on each, distilling them to the basics. That way we'll have the best of the current crop at our fingertips. I'll also volunteer to go online and check out the various resources available to us."

"Please," said Frances. "No online dating. I tried that for about two months and gave up. Every guy I went out with posted a picture that was at least ten years old and forty pounds less. And don't even get me started on their hair!"

"Don't tell me!" said Michelle in mock horror. "The dreaded Trump comb-over!"

We all laughed at that, then got back on track.

"Nope," I said. "Nothing online, I think we have to get out into the field and really see these guys. Do battle." I knew these metaphors could get old quickly, but still I liked them.

"We have to *smell* them," Ariel said. "Some research I was reading said that one of the greatest findings in a happy marriage was that each partner liked the way the other one smelled."

"I'll go with that," I said.

"You should," Ariel shot back. "You probably have the best chance of any of us, you always smell like food."

"I just dab some vanilla behind my ears and some bacon fat between my breasts," I said. "After all, the way to a man's heart…" Everyone laughed.

We were laughing and happy that Saturday evening after our book group, the fire crackling, the smell of coffee in the air, the cats and dog lying contentedly in our laps, as we anticipated what lay ahead.

"*This* one?" Frances said the following morning, staring at the box of hair coloring. She turned to Michelle. "It looks too dark."

"Trust me," said Michelle. "With your coloring, it'll be fantastic. And I know just the makeup to match."

"Okay," said Frances, tossing it into the red plastic basket.

I strolled along after the two of them, content to watch for now. Frances had talked privately to Michelle before we'd disbanded the night before and asked her if she could help her with hair coloring. She knew her color wasn't as good as it could be, but wasn't sure what to do.

"What a laugh, huh?" she'd said. "Here I've been painting with oils half my life and I can't figure out my own hair color."

"It's always harder to do this for yourself," Michelle said soothingly. I could see why she was such a success at what she did. If anyone had an exclusive on being insecure, it was an actor. So much of their job boiled down to how they looked, and Michelle could convince anyone that either they looked just fine or things could be improved.

Frances had asked Michelle if she could come early on Sunday, before the meeting, and we could zip over to Rite Aid and get her hair dye, then start it up so she'd be drying her newly dyed hair before anyone else arrived. That way, she could move right into makeup. I admired that quality in Frances. She usually made up her mind in a heartbeat, then jumped right in. If we were going to work on self-improvement, on looking better, then she was going for it all the way.

"Sure," Michelle had said. It was one of the qualities she had that I just adored. Here she was, in the middle of her own intense heartbreak, her entire world falling apart, and she was willing to help someone else.

Another thing that I admired about Michelle was that, aside from her one outburst the previous evening about her husband and never dating again, she wasn't putting a damper on anything that was going on. She knew that what we all needed more than anything was hope, and she wasn't going to crush things for any of us.

"Didn't you want to update some of your makeup, Eva? Maybe a few new colors?" Michelle said, and I started realizing she was talking to me.

"Yeah," I replied. "Whatever you think would be good for me, just throw it in the basket."

"Same here," said Frances.

"You know what I might do?" said Michelle. "While you guys start the meeting with Wendy and Ariel, I might get a list from both of them of what they'd like to change in their hair and makeup and come over here and do a little more shopping. That would save you guys some time."

"Sounds like a plan," said Frances. She'd taken the box of coloring out of the basket again and was studying it, and it looked as if she was getting herself used to going with just a little darker shade of red.

Wendy and Ariel arrived right on time, at noon, and so our first meeting began.

"Okay," I said, taking a bamboo knitting needle and tapping it on the surface of the coffee table. "The first *really* official meeting of the I Hate to Date Club has begun!"

Clapping and raucous cheers greeted this announcement, and I had to laugh. Shaking my head in bemusement, I sat back in one of the overstuffed chairs. The weather outside was gorgeous, cool and clear without a hint of rain. We'd opted for another fire, even though we didn't really need it. It just made the room cozier. I'd piled up the afghans and pillows so we'd be really comfy.

"I picked this up for you yesterday on the way home, Eva," Ariel said, reaching into her large tote bag and

pulling out a paperback book. She tossed me a copy of
Winter Solstice. "I figured if you got the book really early,
there was a chance you might actually finish reading it!"

"You don't read Paige's selections?" Frances said, in
mock horror.

Wendy's beautiful eyes widened.

"That's okay, I've missed a few myself," Frances confessed.

"Cliff's Notes?" I said.

"And the movies," Frances said.

Now I knew the group was going to work. We were
definitely all on the same page.

Everyone had oohed and aahed over Frances's new
hair color. She was a natural redhead, as she'd explained
to Michelle, but her hair had begun to fade and some
gray had come in, so she'd started coloring it. But she'd
always felt that the color wasn't quite right.

"I know it looks dark now," Michelle had said to her
when she'd first taken the towel off Frances's head and
looked at the wet strands. "But when it's dry, it'll look
fantastic. We could even add some subtle highlighting."

I'd made a chicken-and-dumpling-type casserole,
along with green beans and homemade rolls. I'd wanted
a comfort food feel to the meal. Wendy had told me
she'd supply dessert, and had brought a truly decadent
cake from Gelson's.

So here we were, Frances finishing blowing out her hair, Michelle shaping Ariel's brows, and Wendy in the kitchen with me, helping me serve up the meal. She seemed quiet, withdrawn, and I stopped dishing up the casserole at the stove.

"Want to talk about it?" I offered.

She looked about as miserable as a woman could look.

"Eva, I'm going to need some help," she said.

"What do you need? You know we're all here for you."

Wendy paused and seemed to reconsider what she'd been just about to say.

"Just spit it out. Don't think about it. Go with the flow."

"I'm going to need some real help getting away from him."

My stomach plummeted. "Is he violent?"

"No, no, nothing like that. It's me. I don't know what's wrong with me, but it's almost as if I'm addicted to him. We've been out so many times and I've felt that I had to end the whole thing, and I just—I can't seem to do it."

An idea was forming in my mind. "Can you stay a little later today?"

"Sure."

"There's a DVD that I want you to watch."

We had lunch by the fireplace, around the coffee table like last night. Everyone really loved the casserole, especially when I told them that I'd reworked the original recipe and made it a little more low-fat.

"Not nonfat," I said decisively. "That stuff blows. But it's amazing what you can get away with when you go low. Just a few tricks."

So we talked and ate and laughed, and everyone admired Frances's new hair color and Ariel's new brows.

"I should have you do mine next," I said to Michelle.

"You're the only one left. I did Frances and Ariel, and Wendy's are perfection."

Michelle did a brief makeover talk about makeup, offered her professional opinion about what each of us could do, then volunteered to go to the drugstore and purchase a few things for Ariel and Wendy. But no one wanted her to leave just yet.

"You're part of this group," Wendy said. "We need your advice when we talk about our lists."

I could tell Michelle was pleased.

Ariel pushed her plate aside and said, "Let's get to the lists."

"Biggest assets and stumbling blocks," Frances said. "You first."

"Okay." Ariel pulled a steno pad out of her tote bag and flipped it open.

"Assets. I'm smart, I have a good mind, and people

tend to warm up to me quickly. I don't suffer fools. I know what I'm doing at my job—"

"What do you do again?" Michelle said.

"I work at a publishing house in Santa Monica. And—" here she glanced at me, then turned to everyone else and said "—I'm working on a screenplay in my spare time. I've finished two that were pretty bad, but I think I really have something with this third one!"

Everyone clapped.

"I don't tell many people about my writing. Just my writing partner, Nate."

"Any potential for a relationship there?" said Frances.

"He treats me like a buddy," Ariel said.

"Could you like him?" Frances said, pressing her case.

Ariel thought for a moment, then said, "Yeah. I could."

Michelle grabbed a notebook of mine that I'd put out to take notes and began writing.

"More assets," I called out.

"I was ready to go on to stumbling blocks," Ariel admitted.

"How about we, as objective onlookers, talk about some of Ariel's assets," said Michelle. "I do it all the time, sizing up clients I'm going to work on. Did you know that quite a few actresses have eyes that are different colors?"

"Really?" said Wendy.

"Jane Seymour for one, and that girl who was in *Blue Crush*, the surfing movie, Kate something. And they both turned it into an asset."

"Okay," said Ariel. "I'm tough. Fire away!"

I laughed and she looked at me and said, "What?"

"You're such a little scrapper!"

"That's the trouble!" Ariel burst out. "I feel sometimes like I'm so small that no one takes me seriously!"

"That can be fixed," Michelle said, still writing furiously. "You know what I see?"

"What?" Ariel looked intrigued.

"You have a body most women would die for, petite and curvy, but strong. Eva's told me you have a great metabolism and can eat all you want. You have gorgeous coloring, that dark hair and pale skin, and those dark eyes. You can wear much stronger colors than you've been wearing, especially lipstick or gloss. And you could dress stronger, it might help people notice you."

"How do you mean?" Now Ariel was intrigued.

"You're so small, your clothes have to fit perfectly. You need to find a good tailor and make him or her your new best friend. I'd suggest some really sexy power suits for work. Do you have a writers' group, or is Nate your only writer friend?"

"There's a group, six of us. We all took a class through

UCLA Extension and decided to keep working together after it ended. I'm the only woman. I met Nate there and we partnered off."

"Hmm," said Frances. She looked at me and smiled and I knew what she was thinking.

"So they treat you like someone's little sister?" Michelle asked.

"Like I'm the friggin' mascot!" Ariel said.

"Okay." Michelle stopped writing and studied the notebook in front of her. "With your coloring, you should be wearing jewel-like tones and very pale, almost icy pastels. Is that what's in your wardrobe?"

"The pastels, yeah. But not the jewel tones. I thought dark colors would make me look even smaller."

"Depends. Do you wear makeup when you meet with the boys?"

Ariel hesitated, then said, "No. Most of the time I'm so tired by Saturday that I just haul my ass out of bed, pull on jeans and a sweatshirt, comb my hair and I'm out the door. We meet for exactly two hours and then we're on our way."

"And *that's*," said Michelle, "why they treat you like their little sister."

Silence as we all digested this.

"I work on films," Michelle said quietly. "It's all about illusion, about what you present to people in order to make them feel specific emotions. It's not manipulation, though I suppose you could look at it that way. But if you want a particular result, you have to work for it."

"Wow," said Frances.

"I do makeup. Someone else does costumes. Someone else creates the set. All of it's done with an eye toward character. So what all of you have to do is decide what character you want to be at any given time. For example, you, Ariel, would be different at work than with the boys."

"They'd laugh their asses off if I wore a power suit to our meeting," said Ariel. "We meet at a coffee shop in West Hollywood at nine that's central to all of us."

"Yeah," said Michelle. "I understand. But what's to say that there might have to be a little subterfuge involved?"

Ariel was quiet for a moment, then leaned forward. "I'm listening."

"What if you came to one of your screenplay meetings in a full-on power suit, just exquisite, with power makeup, high heels, the whole works. What if you blew into that meeting just a little late, said you were sorry but you had an early breakfast business meeting that came up suddenly and you ran a little late?"

"I get it," said Ariel.

"Do those guys know anything about the publishing business?"

"No."

"That's perfect, then. Ariel, sometimes you have to shake people up, get them to see you in different ways so that they can respond to you differently. I'll give you a classic example. A beautiful actress gets parts because of that beauty, but no one thinks she can act her way out of a barrel. So she gets a part where she wears no makeup, or very little, has dirt on her face, or lets her hair get all scraggy and, voila! Academy Award!"

"*Norma Rae*," Wendy said softly.

"*Monster*," I added.

"It's not that it was only the look," Michelle said. "I don't want to imply that at all, it would be an insult to the actresses. Sally Field and Charlize Theron were both terrific actresses before they got the roles. But the different look really made the industry sit up and take notice."

"So what you're saying," Frances said, "is that we could do the same in our lives. If we wanted a certain response, we could dress a certain way, do certain things, to make us receive an almost guaranteed response."

"Exactly. It puts the power squarely in your hands."

"Okay!" said Ariel, and I could tell she was really excited by this new idea. Ariel and ideas went together; she had a great mind. She was a powerhouse that people routinely underestimated because of her size. It had been a great frustration to her since I've known her, and now she saw a way out.

"In a nutshell," Ariel said, addressing all of us, "my problem is my size. People overlook me or think of me as this little sister. I want to sex it up, I want to get some power going, I want to be a woman to be reckoned with!"

"Easy," Michelle said. "Stronger makeup, feminine power suits, higher heels. Some really good classic jewelry, but not too much because you'd be overpowered. I can give you names of designers who would be good for your body type. And try that trick of coming from a meeting to your group—blow their minds, Ariel. Nate might wake up and look at you in a whole new way. Besides, you'll get some looks at the coffee shop—"

"We *are* talking West Hollywood here," I interjected, and everyone started to laugh.

"Hey, gay men appreciate fashion more than almost anyone else," Michelle said. "Any attention from any man will get another man going, it's just the way it is."

"So you're set to go, Ariel?" I said.

"Yeah!" She was busily making notes in her steno pad. "I want Michelle to show me how to do my makeup, then give me names so I can go shopping. I'm going to try all of this out before our next meeting!"

"So next Saturday morning, you could have a breakfast meeting with an author, or a client or something," I said. "And wear the suit."

"Exactly," said Wendy and Michelle together.

"And," said Wendy, "you have to make a commitment to an early night, and then get up that morning with enough time to make sure you look absolutely stunning."

I was sure Wendy knew all about early nights and difficult locations, bad weather, everything that went with the life of a model. Perks too, of course.

"And a little bit of acting," I said, "running into the meeting and looking all flustered because you're about ten minutes late. But make sure you have the story locked and loaded, how the fake meeting went and all that stuff, how you couldn't get away, blah-blah-blah."

"Excellent," said Ariel, still taking notes. "This gives me a great assignment to get done before our next meeting. I'm totally happy with this, guys! I'm going to look on it as a grand experiment, and I'll report back."

"All right," I said, turning to Frances. "Next!"

We went a lot later than we thought, but no one objected. The sky slowly darkened outside, I added another log to the fire, but no one seemed to want to go home just yet.

Everyone was taking things to a different level and at a different speed. Frances just wanted to work on her looks. She told us she'd divorced her husband two years ago and the first year alone had been absolute hell. She'd thought of herself as a total failure.

I watched Michelle's face as Frances said this and could tell Michelle knew exactly what she was talking about. She was thinking about what she was in for. I've never been married, so I can't say I know what both of them had experienced. There was something about making a real commitment with a man and then watching him break it that did terrible things to a woman.

Anyway, Frances was already happy. She loved her new hair color now that it was dry, and I had to admit that it was a great improvement over the original. She and Michelle were debating whether to do highlights, but would wait until the following meeting. Frances had written down the color that Michelle had bought for her, and had chosen to use her time in the group for Michelle to do an actual makeover with her, using the cosmetics she'd bought earlier.

Her assets? She'd written down that her biggest asset was having the strength to survive her divorce with no real support from family and just a few close friends. We were all astonished to discover that Frances had been a high-powered lawyer who had met her husband at the firm. Once the divorce had shattered her, she'd reassessed her entire life, left the law firm where she'd been racking up incredibly long hours, and changed everything.

She still practiced law, but now at a smaller firm that was particular about the cases they took. She worked part-time, had a life outside work and had thrown herself into her first love, painting.

"What my divorce made me realize was that life is way too short to keep putting off your dreams."

"Very wise," Wendy said. I could still see that sadness in her eyes.

When Michelle finished the makeover, we were all astonished at the change in Frances. Michelle had done several looks for her, and Frances had asked Ariel to take notes for her. One for day, another for work, and a third and final look for a glamorous evening out.

"You look beautiful," Wendy told her.

"Stunning," I said.

"I have this gallery opening later in the week," Frances said as she studied herself in the hand mirror I'd given her. "Would I want to do the evening look?"

"What time is the opening?" Michelle asked.

"Seven in the evening."

"Go for the glamour," Michelle advised. "Is it the sort of thing where champagne is served? Food?"

"Yeah."

"Wear black, it will set off your new hair color, and do the evening makeup just like I showed you. And talk with as many people, men and women, as you can."

"Can this count as my date?" Frances asked. "I've been a hermit since my divorce, so I don't really know too many men who would ask me out."

I sensed she wasn't trying to make excuses, simply easing herself back into the dating pool. She'd made a brave stab at it with the online dating and that had been a bust. I thought that, considering all the change Frances had been through today, it would be fine.

"I'm okay with that," I said. "How about everyone else?"

"I believe," said Ariel, "this whole looks thing that Michelle explained to us is so profound that I think we should all try it out this week. We should take a stab at pretending to be the women we eventually want to be, and do it in a public arena. It'll get our confidence up so that we'll be ready for that first date."

You just don't want to date, I almost said. Then I saw the look in Frances's eyes and hesitated.

"So," I said. "Everyone okay with Ariel just doing the screenwriting meeting and Frances the gallery opening?"

Everyone agreed.

"You're happy with everything, Frances?"

"Oh, yeah."

"Then," said Ariel, looking directly at me. "I think Eva's next."

CHAPTER 6

The *moment of truth.*

If I'm honest with myself, I've always used humor to get myself out of difficult situations. I could remember the exact moment on the grade-school playground when I'd realized that if I made the class bully laugh, he wouldn't pound me into the asphalt. And I have been riding that particular pony my entire life.

But this time, humor wouldn't cut it.

I'd made out my list, and when I'd first thought about "biggest assets," I'd considered getting a laugh by saying that I looked like Meg Ryan with boobs. Over the years, I've gotten used to guys talking to my chest. If a man even met my eyes when he talked to me, he went up a few points on my secret scorecard.

My sister Meg and I both inherited our mother's build. I was never one of those girls who wondered when their breasts would develop. Knowing that I took after my mother, I simply waited for the mother lode.

But now I knew I couldn't play it for laughs. I had to bite the bullet and tell the truth.

"Biggest assets," I began. "I'm a really good cook. I'm not that hard on the eyes. I have a soft heart, I'm loyal to a fault, I love animals, and while I'm not that courageous in my own life, I'll go to the mat for a friend."

"Yep," said Michelle.

"I own my own home, I'm okay with money, not too much debt, I really like people. I'm well read except for the books in our group that I choose not to read, I think I would be a fun date. I have all my teeth—"

Come on, I couldn't resist. Everyone laughed, but Ariel gave me a stern look and I knew I couldn't get away with another joke.

"—I love movies and carnivals and food festivals and I'm open to trying other things. I'm not that judgmental, I try not to judge at all, and I really, really want to find a good man and settle down into being a couple. Because I'm a lot more happy as part of a couple, I like doing things as part of a team. I miss not having a man in my life."

I stopped, winded by my speech, and looked up at the circle of women. I didn't feel judged at all, just sensed the warmth and caring coming from them.

Talk about synchronicity. All of us coming together at the same time, for the same reason. I'd been friends with Michelle my whole life, with Ariel for most of it, and Frances and Wendy had fit right in.

"As for biggest stumbling blocks," I began.

"Ah ah ah! No, we have a few things to add," said Ariel. "You're the whole reason this group was born. You were the one who offered us a place to meet and a pan of lasagna. It's no mistake that Wendy asked if she could talk to you after our book group. You're one of the most caring people I know, and I'm not surprised that your caring overflowed into a career of making fabulous food for people. You're an incredible friend, we've all seen how your house is like a second home to the people you love—"

Michelle nodded her head.

"—but the point I'm trying to make is that I have never, *ever*, seen you see a need and not do something to fill it. You're unique, Eva, and I love you for it."

"She's right," Wendy joined in. "A lot of people see other people's pain and just say and do nothing. They hope it'll go away and it won't have to touch them."

"I really appreciate what you've done for me so far, Eva," said Frances. "I've come to know all of you so much better than just from the reading group. I have a new hair color and makeup I love, I'm not too intimidated to go to this gallery opening, and I have a group that makes me feel a hell of a lot better about facing what's out there.

So, you go girl! You rock!" And she held up her glass of wine.

The others did the same, and I have to say it was a great feeling.

"Now that that's out of the way, we can get on to those stumbling blocks," Ariel said with a twinkle in her dark eyes.

"Okay," I said. "I'm clueless about how to go about finding a guy. I'm getting older. I work in a field dominated by women or gay men. If I'd wanted to meet a man, I should've become a professional chef. The thing is, most of the social stuff in a family is still planned by women, so I'm usually meeting with women to plan weddings, brunches, baby showers, family reunions, all that stuff. Occasionally a man will want to plan a romantic dinner for his girlfriend or wife, but obviously he's already happy, and taken."

All the women were listening attentively.

"Now, I know Michelle will tell you that she's invited me to countless parties, as has Ariel. And I guess the thing is, what you need to know about me is that I'm in a really dangerous time of my life. I'm in my late thirties and I'm tired of dating. I'm kind of that woman who, given a choice between a good thriller and a great cup of coffee and going out for a night on the town and a couple of parties—I'll pick the book and the coffee."

"Curled up in bed," Ariel said. "Lots of pillows."

"A real page-turner," Michelle said.

"And maybe some chocolate," I added. "What I'm trying to say is that I've literally been dating more than half of my life. And I feel like Charlotte in that episode of *Sex and the City* where she said, 'Where the hell is he? Where's that guy that was supposed to show up and begin our happily-ever-after?'" To my embarrassment, I felt tears welling up in my eyes. But I forged ahead.

"I've had sequential relationships, but any time I was asked to get married I wasn't ready, I didn't feel it was the right time. Maybe I was scared, I don't know. But all I know is that I want to have a relationship progress beyond the old living-together-and-being-a-couple point. I want a man to love me enough to build a future with me. Because I think I could be a really wonderful wife!"

"Yeah, you could," Michelle said, reaching over to take my hand.

"But I'm clueless, guys, and a hopeless romantic. So any help you can give me, I'd be so grateful for." For just a moment after I finished, I felt so vulnerable, so completely exposed.

Then Frances said, "I feel the same way, Eva, and I've actually been married."

Michelle was blinking rapidly. I think what I'd said

had really gotten to her. "Me, too. I'm not even out of my marriage and I'm already wishing for something I don't think I ever really had with my husband, if I'm honest."

Wendy had reached for the tissue box, and Ariel was staring down at her steno pad.

"I think," she said, "that you just put into words what the rest of us feel. And precisely why we have to put together a battle plan."

I was so grateful for their support that I didn't even realize she'd used one of my war metaphors.

"Isn't it all a numbers game?" Ariel said. "Aren't our odds improved every time we go out to that party and resist the temptation to curl up with a book or watch our favorite television show?"

"Yeah," said Frances, cradling her wineglass in her hands. "But it depends on the party." She thought for a moment, then said, "I can get all of you on the list for this gallery opening later this week. I mean, there might not be anyone, but there could be."

"Numbers," said Ariel. "I could throw a little party at my condo and invite all the men I know from my screenwriting classes, and even ask them to bring friends. Really casual with these guys, jeans and sweaters and a pot of spaghetti, that type of thing. Maybe you could help me come up with some great food, Eva. But we just need to create situations where we're around a bunch of men!"

"No knitting groups, huh, Eva?" Michelle said, giving me a pointed look.

"I know!" I said. "Everything I do is kind of female-centric. But I don't feel right about joining an investment club or an antique car club just to meet men if I have no interest in those things. It's kind of like a lie."

"What do you mean, kind of?" said Frances. "It *is* a lie. No, between the five of us, we've got to be able to generate enough invites that we can all go out and hunt for that guy on a regular basis. But casually, of course. Nothing smells worse than desperation."

"But Eva," said Michelle quietly. "You have to make that commitment to go out to every single social engagement you're asked to, instead of holing up at home with that book."

"I know," I said. "I agree with you, I've been bad and I really want to change and I need you guys to help me."

"So, what's your problem?" Wendy said. "Do men see you as a sister, or a caretaker, or what?"

"I have to be really careful because of what I do. Cooking food can come across as such a mom thing, like an earth mother or a caretaker. I have to watch out for men who just want mothers, and I wouldn't want that kind of guy."

"What image would you want to portray?" Frances asked. "'Cause I'm telling you, this hair is going to make me want to act a little differently. It's always good to mix it up."

"So who are you, Eva?" Ariel said. "Ginger or Mary Ann? Scarlett or Melanie? Samantha or Miranda or Charlotte or Carrie?"

"All great feminine icons," Wendy said.

"Well, I'm not Ginger—" I began.

"I beg to differ," said Frances. "You have quite a little figure there, Eva."

"Yeah, but—it's not me."

"If you say that you're Mary Ann because she used to bake those coconut-cream pies, so help me I'll smack you," said Michelle.

"No, not Mary Ann. I don't cook all the time, and believe me, I'm not that wholesome. And I'm not Scarlett, I'm not that ambitious. I'm not as noble or good as Melanie—who is?—and I'm not as sexually driven as Samantha. I'm not as rigid and perfectionist as Miranda, in no way am I as romantic as Charlotte—"

"—so that leaves Carrie," said Ariel.

"Except that I don't smoke and don't write that well. Or at least I've never tried. So, guys, where's my Mr. Big?"

"Remember how Carrie met him?" said Ariel. "At a party or a club or something."

"She got out of her apartment," Michelle said.

"Point taken," I replied.

"I'm just as bad as you are, Eva," said Ariel. "Only with me, it's work. I stay late at my job, I take manuscripts home, and before I know it, a week, a month, half a year has gone by and I haven't even gone out anywhere!"

"This is why this group is so good," Wendy said. "We can encourage each other."

"So, if you're Carrie," said Ariel to me, then turning to Michelle, "what should she do about how she presents herself?"

"Oh boy," said Michelle. "I know just the changes she should make, 'cause I've been bugging her to make them for years!"

I knew what was coming.

"Highlights in her hair, slightly bolder makeup. She's got that girl-next-door thing going on, but she's got to sex it up or guys consider her a friend. Eva's the kind of woman that you might not drop your jaw when you see her, but by the end of the evening, she's the one you want to leave the party with. After a conversation with her, a guy forgets all the superficial pretties in the room. We just have to get her to that party, and I just have to get her to the point where jaws *do* drop when she walks in."

"I love it!" said Ariel.

"And one other very important point I'd like to make," Michelle said. "Those superficial pretty girls use every beauty trick in the book to look fantastic. The only two working actresses I've made up so far in my career who are genuinely drop-dead gorgeous without any help are Nicole Kidman and Faith Hill. They both have gorgeous skin and perfect features. So a lot is attainable with the right makeup, hair and clothing. And anyway, don't most people look better with a little makeup?"

"Okay," Ariel said suddenly, and she reached into her large tote bag. For a tiny woman, Ariel carries around a lot of stuff. But it's always carefully thought out. She pulled out a huge calendar for the new year, and as we were right in January at the present moment, her timing couldn't have been better.

"Guys," she said, her hand back inside her bag, "pick a color."

"Pink," said Michelle.

"Green," I said.

"Blue," said Wendy.

"Red," said Frances.

"And I'll take yellow. What we're going to do is list all the things we're committing to do. And all the invites we're generating. For example, Frances, what night is the gallery opening?"

"Thursday."

"Okay. So I'm going to write that in on this Thursday in red because Frances was responsible for generating that invitation for all of us, and because it really is her assignment. How does that sound?"

"Fantastic!" I said, and I had to admit I was really impressed, but not surprised. Ariel always comes prepared.

"Okay, the invites for all of us will be circled," she said, and did so on the night of the gallery opening. "Saturday, in the morning, is my screenwriting group. So I'll write it down in yellow—it's something that I've committed to, the whole power-suit thing. Shaking Nate up."

We watched as she wrote in: "Power Suit Screenplay Group."

"There. Now I've committed to that. It's not something where all of you can come along, but it still moves me closer to our goal of all of us having wonderful relationships with fantastic men. See?"

"Can I come to the gallery opening?" Michelle said. "Not to date but just to get out of the house. And I really do like art."

"Of course you can," said Frances. "It'll be good for your mental health. Don't do like I did and take sick days and hole up at home and eat chocolate. I think I watched every romantic movie that AMC had to offer, it was the only way I could really let loose and cry."

"Gallery openings are better," I agreed.

"So, Eva," Ariel said, picking up the green marker. I practically quailed inside; she reminded me of a grade-school teacher who scared the crap out of me. But this was only Ariel, and she wanted what was best for me.

"Eva," Ariel continued. "You're going out to the gallery this Thursday with the rest of us, and considering that your biggest date so far this year, or even all of last year, has been with a copy of *The Da Vinci Code* and an espresso, this is a definite improvement. So that can count as your date. But—"

I knew there was a *but*. There always is.

"But you have to commit to a day when Michelle can do your highlights, maybe a new hairstyle, and new makeup. And it has to be before Thursday night. And she also gets to check out the outfit you're planning to wear. You cannot play it safe. None of us can. There's no time to lose."

Ariel was really getting fired up about all this. As I knew there was absolutely no escape, and as a part of me was desperate for a change in my life, I nodded my head.

"Is that enough for Eva?" Ariel said to the group at large.

"I think that's fine for now," Frances said. She caught my look and said, "I would say the same about me."

"Okay," said Ariel, setting the huge wall calendar to

the side of the coffee table. "We can hang this calendar up in Eva's kitchen and then take it down for each group meeting and make sure we all kept our word and did what we committed to. Okay?"

Everyone agreed.

"Do you feel like you're done, Eva?" said Wendy.

"More like done for. No, I'm fine, we can move on."

Everyone's attention centered on Wendy, and for a moment she looked so much like a terrified deer staring into headlights. But she rallied, and began to speak.

"I don't know if talking about my biggest assets and stumbling blocks is the right thing to do at this point in time. I actually wanted to ask the three of you—even the four of you—if you'd all help me with something that's going to take a lot out of me."

I knew what she was going to ask us to do, and I was ready.

"I need to break up with this guy," she said softly, then her eyes filled and she swiped at the tears with one hand. We all waited, giving her the courtesy of time, letting her tell us what needed to be said in her own way.

"I can't do this anymore. I can't. He's never going to leave his wife, he's never going to want to be with me. And how could I ever trust him when I know he cheated on his wife with me? I should've walked away the moment I found out he was married."

"When did he tell you?" Frances asked.

"Six months into the relationship."

"So he lied?" Michelle asked.

"No, it was never an issue, he didn't wear a ring. I just assumed—I was so damn stupid."

"No," said Michelle, and I could see she was thinking about her husband and how he'd cheated on her with his twentysomething mistress. "No, don't go there. You have to start from where you are. What do you need us to do?"

"It's—this Wednesday night, we're meeting for dinner. I'm going to break up with him, but I was thinking—if you all were there, at another table, and I felt your support—"

"You got it," said Frances, glancing around the room.

"I can make it," said Ariel.

"I'll be there," I said.

"Me, too," said Michelle.

"But I want to pay for your dinner, he's taking me to a pretty expensive place—"

The name she gave us almost caused my jaw to drop. A stunningly expensive and exclusive Italian restaurant in Santa Monica. I knew there was a waiting list for reservations a mile long, so how did this guy rate? He must have had a connection somewhere. And Wendy was right. This restaurant was way out of our price range.

"I won't agree to any of you coming unless you allow me to pay for your dinner. I'll give you cash. I had some incredible jobs last year, and I can afford it. It would mean so much to me if you were all there."

"Of course," Ariel said, whipping out that calendar again. "This Wednesday?"

"Yes."

"What time?"

"Seven."

"How can we get a reservation?" Frances asked, exactly what I was thinking myself.

"I have a friend who works there, one of the waiters. He'll pull a few strings for me."

Suddenly I understood. Wendy probably didn't have a whole lot of close female friends, not the way she looked. Her waiter friend was probably gay, and she'd asked her married man to take her to that particular restaurant so she'd have a friend in case she fell apart.

Now she had four more.

"I'll be right in Santa Monica after work," said Ariel. "Do you want me to come and pick you up?"

"Would you?"

I was so glad Ariel had suggested it. I knew I wouldn't be in any shape to drive back home if I were finishing up a relationship that had meant so much to me, no matter what it had meant to him.

"Why don't we all meet at your place, Ariel?" Frances suggested. "We can park our cars there, get in just one, then pick up Wendy and head to the restaurant together. We'll drop you off in front, then park the car and the rest of us can go in together."

I looked at Frances with a whole new level of respect. She'd make a hell of a general.

"I don't have to go if it's that expensive," said Michelle.

"No," said Wendy. "I'd like all of you there. You've been such a help to me. It's been good for me, listening to all of you, because that's been my greatest fear. That if I break up with this man I'll have to start searching for someone all over again."

But you don't even really have him, I thought, but kept it to myself.

Ariel wrote in the place and time, then circled it in blue. So this was another group endeavor, but we weren't exactly going to go looking for eligible men. We were helping Wendy extricate herself from the man she was already with.

"What's the signal if you need our help?" I asked.

"I'll pull on my earlobe, the way Carol Burnett used to do on her show. Then I'll head for the ladies' room and you can meet me there."

"Sounds like a plan," said Frances.

We discussed it just a little more, then Ariel, our un-official secretary with her large calendar, gave us a recap.

After she was finished, we all gave her the thumbs-up sign.

"Eva is going to let Michelle highlight her hair—when?" Ariel asked.

I glanced at Michelle.

"Tomorrow?" she said. "I'm between films."

"I don't have a catering job until Tuesday afternoon."

"Monday it is," said Ariel, writing it into the large square with the green pen that was my personal color.

"I'm in your hands," I told Michelle. And this was good, because if she was busy working on me, she had less time to worry about her upcoming divorce.

"And Wendy," Ariel continued, "looks so damn gorgeous she doesn't need a makeover, but she'll be at the restaurant on Wednesday ready to make a major change in her life. That's all you have to do for the *month*, okay?"

Wendy nodded, looking spent. There was thinking about breaking off a relationship, and then there was actually deciding to do it. It was tough, but I knew it was the best thing for her.

"And Michelle?" Ariel said.

"What?" said Michelle. "I'm just helping you guys out."

"No, you've done an awful lot for us. I want you to come prepared to the next meeting and ask us to do something for you."

"Really?" I could tell this touched my friend deeply.

"Yep," said Ariel. "You made the meeting, with our makeovers. You wouldn't have time to go by the Rite Aid after the meeting, would you? Like you said, I need more color in my life!"

"I'd love to. We can even come back here and I'll show you some tricks."

Our first meeting came to an end. We clinked wine-glasses, drank the tiny bit of wine that was left and began to go back to our own lives. Frances left first. I could tell she was still so jazzed over her new hair. Then Michelle and Ariel took off for the drugstore. They'd also talked about stopping by Sephora on Colorado Boulevard if it was still open.

That left Wendy and me.

"Did you still want to watch that DVD?" she said. "I can just borrow it and take it home if you want."

This woman was so used to taking crumbs. And she had a hellish week ahead; she needed all the support we could offer her.

"I'd love to see it with you. That is, unless you have to get home."

"No. No, I'd love to stay."

"Okay."

I made sure the screen was securely in front of the dying fire, then made us some more coffee, cut us each another thin slice of the decadently rich chocolate-mousse cake she'd brought, and settled us back in my small library.

It was never supposed to be a library. It was actually a really huge dining room that opened out from the kitchen. But the kitchen had a breakfast nook, which was where I usually ate, and as it sat six, I'd decided that I probably wouldn't use the dining room all that often. If I had that many people over, I could do a buffet and spill out into the living room.

I'd put in a bunch of bookshelves, two really comfy squishy chairs, a couple of lamps and an entertainment center complete with television, DVD player and a stereo. It was cozy and quiet and ideal for what I had in mind.

"Have you ever seen this movie?" I said, passing her the DVD.

"No," she said, handing it back to me. "What's it about?"

"Believe it or not, quantum physics and relationships."

Wendy looked doubtful. "Will I be able to under-stand it?"

"Yeah, they did a great job. And the great thing about watching it this way is that if there's something you don't get, we can go back as much as you want. It blew my mind when I saw it, and I think it's the perfect film for where you're at."

So Wendy settled back in her chair and reached for her coffee, and I slipped my copy of *What the Bleep Do We Know?* into the DVD player.

We watched the entire movie, and as always, once it was done, there were so many things to talk about, so many questions to ask.

"So," Wendy said, "what scientists are saying is that our cells use the same receptor sites to receive chemical emotional signals as heroin?"

"Yes."

"So I'm literally *addicted* to this man?"

"Exactly. Remember that squishy thing in the animated part about the brain? The hypothalamus? It released the neuropeptides that went zinging toward the cell sites, and that's where the addiction to a specific feeling comes from. Or the addiction to a drug."

"So by hooking up with this guy, I'm addicted to feeling sad in relationships?"

"Got it in one. I had a friend who was always angry. We went to see this movie together when it first came out, and he walked out of the theater and said, 'That's it, I'm done.'"

"Really. Did it take?"

"Yeah. It's powerful, super empowering stuff, when

you really know how your body works and how it can shape your worldview. To me, it helps a person evolve."

I'd brought out some cheese and crackers to offset the sugar high from the chocolate-mousse cake, and now Wendy and I were sitting in my little library, discussing the movie.

"That's exactly what it feels like with him, like an addiction."

"Have you tried to break up with him before?" I knew this was crucial information to have before the big night on Wednesday. The more we knew, the more we could help Wendy get out of this emotional mess.

"Twice."

This was not good. "What happened?"

"He called and begged me to come back, and I caved in. I'm weak."

"No. Let's keep going with the addict metaphor." Boy, did I like metaphors! "If you're addicted to him, you need to quit cold turkey. If you stay away from him for a certain amount of time, it'll get easier."

"How am I going to do that when he'll start calling all the time?"

"We'll think of something," I said just as Ariel and Michelle walked in. Ariel was sporting her new much more sexy and colorful look, and both Wendy and I jumped up, amazed.

"You look *great!*" I said.

"No more little sister, that's for sure," said Ariel. "And Michelle gave me another great suggestion for not becoming one of the guys—perfume! I never would've thought of it, but she said it only takes a few seconds to put on a really light, feminine scent and a little lipstick. Then they have a *lot* more trouble thinking of you as one of them. I never thought about it, but men really are so visual."

"It's that old hunter thing," I said. "Those woolly mammoths."

"It's all just common sense," Michelle said, but I could tell she was pleased.

Ariel was so excited, she kept talking. "And we're going shopping together this Tuesday evening for that great suit. I need her eye, I have absolutely *no* objectivity when it comes to me." She turned to Michelle, hugged her and said, "You should go into business doing this for people. You're brilliant!"

"Thanks." Michelle looked at Wendy and me. "What did you guys do?"

"Just finished watching *What the Bleep Do We Know?*" I said.

"I *love* that movie. You know, I should watch it again now that I'm in the middle of this whole mess with Bryan. I don't want to make depression a habit." She glanced at Wendy. "And it's a great movie for you to be watching at this time."

We all chatted a little more, then Ariel headed toward the front door, still talking excitedly to Michelle about their upcoming evening of shopping. Wendy got up to go, and I followed her toward the living room.

"Thanks, Eva," she said. "It gave me a whole new way of looking at the relationship. Now I know that I have to end it. Cold turkey."

"It's the only way," I said.

She hesitated. "I have an even bigger favor to ask you."

I already knew what it was. "Yes, you may come and stay here for a couple of days to get over the worst of it. I'll keep your cell phone and Blackberry away from you, I won't let you use my phones, or my computer to e-mail or instant message him. I'll keep you straight."

"It's not so much me calling him. It's more about when he calls me. I know he will. And then I get all weak, that damn addiction thing kicks in—"

"He won't be able to find you here."

CHAPTER 7

How could I so blithely offer Wendy a couple of days of shelter in my home? Easy. As a child I brought every wounded lizard, frog, kitten, chick, puppy and playmate home with me. My mother never gave me any grief because she was exactly the same way. There wasn't a Thanksgiving or a Christmas back in the Midwest when we didn't have a few extra people around the table or sitting by the tree.

Also I have to say that I'm pretty intuitive when it comes to people and I've never had a problem. I just knew Wendy wouldn't abuse the privilege, and that she desperately needed some time away from her married man in order to make a clean break. I had no idea what she was going to do about his messages on her cell phone. I hoped they wouldn't have the ability to throw her completely off track with this breakup.

"She's tried to break up with him twice already?" Ariel said when I called her at work the following morning. I didn't think of this as a breach of confidence, Ariel was super-discreet. Besides, the information was essential to our battle plan this coming Wednesday night. "This could be more complicated than we thought."

"Nah. I feel like she's ready. She just needs our support and a bit of time away from his influence. Remember you told me about that book you read about breakups?"

"Yeah, it sold really well, we were all impressed by how it did."

"What was the recommended time to go absolutely cold turkey on a guy once the breakup was accomplished?" I asked.

"Two months. Sixty days. Nothing—no e-mails, no instant messaging, no phone calls, no carrier pigeons, no psychic connections, nothing. Nada. Zip. No messages from friends, no accidental run-ins, no little trips to give him back his stuff. The author was a real hard-ass about this, but he was absolutely right. And he also recommended that you get a breakup buddy."

"That's right, I remember you telling me it was written by a guy. Well, Wendy has four of us as buddies—five, if you count her waiter friend. And if she stays at the house, she'll have Michelle and me full-time."

"Don't let her pick up any of his messages from her cell

phone. But that's going to be a problem, 'cause how will she get work? Doesn't her agency call her about modeling jobs?"

"Yeah, but she can give them my number for the time being." I said.

"I thought she was only staying with you for two or three days."

"I have a feeling it's going to be closer to a week."

"You're a good friend, Eva."

"You, too. I think we're going to have to be really careful on Wednesday, not let anything take us by surprise."

Ariel sighed. "I don't even know this guy and I can't stand him. What is it with married men that they think they can ruin their family and another woman's life?"

"Yeah, I know. But the real question is, what is it about some women that they have this self-destructive urge to go out with a married man?"

"She didn't know for six months, Eva. That's way more than enough time to get locked in, or to fall in love. And I think the bitch of it is, she really does love him. Hey, it takes two, you can't put all the blame on him, even if that six-month lie sucks."

"I know. That was a shitty thing he did, keeping his ring off. Do you still have that breakup book? Maybe we could get some more tips."

"I've got it somewhere. I'll look for it when I get home," Ariel said.

"Okay. I've got to go, Michelle's getting ready to do my highlights."

"You'll look great!"

I was in the middle of getting my highlights when the doorbell rang. Michelle told me to stay put and ran for the door.

"It's Anna!" she called from the living room.

Anna had come before to visit her dog, Ming, as she did a couple of times a month. It still burned me up that Anna's daughter hadn't had the decency to take in her mother's dog after her mother moved to a retirement home. Too much "trouble" for her, I guess.

But then, Anna's daughter has always struck me as someone who looks out for numero uno, and that was it. I wondered what it would feel like to have a child like that. Not good.

Anna poked her head around the corner. "You look like you're wired up for sound," she said, sounding amused. She was petite, barely five foot one, and just turned seventy-one, though you'd never know it. With her short silvery hair and that elegant Italian bone structure, she looked like she was in her early sixties, sometimes even younger.

It was that bone structure. When I lived in Rome I remember meeting men who looked like they'd just stepped off a Roman coin, their profiles were so perfect.

"Just about. In another ten minutes we'll see the fabulous results!" I actually liked to experiment with my hair. I just got lazy and fell into a rut, like we all did at one point or another in our lives.

"Once we rinse you out, I could take off a couple of inches, get rid of all the dead ends," Michelle offered.

"I'm at your mercy. After all, it's part of my assignment."

"What assignment?" Anna said, coming farther into the kitchen. Her gaze immediately rested on the large calendar gracing one of the walls. "The I Hate to Date Club? This sounds promising."

I didn't mind her curiosity at all. Anna and I got to know each other at one of her daughter's Christmas parties. Afterward, while I was cleaning up, we started talking about food. Then we progressed on to Rome, then the Sistine Chapel, then how gorgeous Florence was, then Venice, then what kind of olive oil was best, and it just snowballed from there.

She's given me some killer recipes her mother taught her and that her daughter had no interest in. I've often thought that Anna and I were separated at birth. She should have been in my family, not hers. She was like that fabulous aunt that all of us always wished we had.

"We formed a group," said Michelle, unwrapping a strand of my hair and taking a careful look. She'd met Anna before, and adored her as much as I do. "I mean, I'm not in it, because I'm in the process of getting a divorce and I don't know if I'll ever be with a man again—"

"You will be," Anna said reassuringly. She'd brought a chair over and sat down, then lifted a very happy Ming into her lap. I always loved seeing the two of them together. In a way, I've never fully considered Ming my dog, because he just went bonkers when he saw Anna. And every time I saw the two of them together, I knew I made the right decision.

"It doesn't feel like it right now," Michelle said, folding the small square of foil around my hair again. She was an amazing makeup artist, but had also picked up a lot of knowledge about hair and skin along the way. Michelle never stopped learning, which was one of the reasons she did such a great job.

"Of course not. You need time. What happened? I'm assuming there was another woman."

"How did you know?" I said flatly.

"Because there usually is. Women are the ones who set off into uncharted territory when they leave a marriage. A man usually has to have another woman in the wings, another place to land."

"You know, that's so true," said Michelle, going over to the kitchen counter and reaching up to get down a mug. "Tea?"

"I'd love some," said Anna. She glanced at me, her dark eyes so alive, like a little girl's. "And I'm hoping you made some biscotti."

"How could I not, when I knew you were coming?" I replied. "In the cookie jar, your favorites, the ones with all the almonds."

So we sat and talked, and within a few minutes Michelle pronounced my hair ready to go and we headed toward the sink.

Then I was back in the chair and Michelle got out her scissors and snipped away while we all caught up. Once my hair was cut and all of the ends were swept off the kitchen floor, we adjourned to the living room with our tea and biscotti.

We used to drink a lot of coffee together until Anna's doctor took her off caffeine. I tried making her decaf, but it just didn't work for her, so now I always offered her tea.

"She wants me to move to another home," Anna said, referring to her daughter. My hair had been blown dry by this time and pronounced finished by Michelle. I had to admit it looked about five hundred percent better than it had before. But my happiness was short-lived in the face of this news.

"What? But you love where you live. Why would she want to move you?"

Anna took another sip of her tea, set it down and said, "It's always about the money."

"Where's this place she wants you to go?" Michelle asked.

"Out in Riverside."

"But then you couldn't—you'd be so far away," I said. I'd been about to say she couldn't walk over and see Ming, but I realized that Anna already had figured that out. Riverside was at least an hour and a half away, and with traffic the drive could be a lot more complicated. And Anna no longer drove. It couldn't compare to being just a few blocks away, within walking distance.

So I tried another angle. "It would be harder for her to visit you."

"My daughter doesn't visit all that often. God forgive me, but I think I'd miss Ming more than I would my own little girl."

And who could blame you, I thought, knowing her daughter as I did.

"Don't you get any say in this?" Michelle asked.

"I do, but she can be hard to deal with when she doesn't get her own way. And without her help, I can't afford the place I'm in now. They just raised the rates again."

It pissed me off, to see Anna being treated this way. It wasn't as if she was a difficult woman. She had a roommate, which made the monthly cost of her retirement home a lot cheaper. I couldn't believe that her daughter could be that stingy. I'd been inside her home, she could easily afford to help her mother out financially.

"But why would she want you all the way out there where she could never come and see you—oh," said Michelle, answering her own question.

"Do you need more care?" I asked Anna. I'd thought about trying to phrase it a little more carefully, but the two of us had talked for so long, we could be blunt with each other. She currently lived in a retirement home, but did she need more in the way of assisted living?

"No. It's just cheaper and, for her, easier. She helps out a little with expenses, so this way she doesn't have to. And it gives her an excuse not to come, the distance and the bother."

It makes it easier for her to excuse the fact that she doesn't go to see her mother. An idea was starting to form in my mind, but I was going to have to present it carefully. And then I thought, *Oh what the hell.*

"Anna," I said. "Why don't you come and live here for a while?"

She was in the midst of picking up another biscotti when she turned and stared at me. "No, I couldn't do that!"

"Why not?" I could see Michelle smiling behind Anna, and I knew she knew exactly what I was up to.

"It's too much of an imposition."

"Why? Is there something I don't know about you? Do you shout and swear like a sailor when you don't get your way? Are you unbelievably picky with your eating habits? Do you hog the bathroom? Tie up the phone?"

"No, but—"

"Are you going to have men over at all hours of the night? Will I have to pound on your bedroom door and tell you to keep it down?"

She laughed at that.

"Okay then," I said, getting out the big guns. "Then don't do it for yourself, do it for Ming. He's going to be miserable and heartbroken without you."

I knew that would work. I could see it in her eyes. The Peke was curled up in her lap, so happy, and Anna hadn't stopped petting him since she'd sat down in the kitchen. She'd carried him into the living room and he'd been firmly stationed on her lap, glued there like a little black piece of Velcro.

Her mouth compressed, she blinked rapidly and looked away. I could tell she was fighting back strong emotion, and she was of a generation that didn't give way to emotion easily.

"You could even help me out," I said. The thing that killed people the quickest was when they no longer felt they were needed. And Anna's daughter had given her that feeling a long time ago.

"How?"

"You know that sauce you make?"

"Eva, I gave you the recipe."

"But it never comes out the same as when you make it!"

She started to smile, but I felt like crying. She reminded me of a proud little bird, and here she was in my living room, sitting up straight in one of my chairs, her little dog in her lap. She had no idea what she'd come to mean to me in just a few years' time. All of my family was back in the Midwest, and I missed them. Anna was always a fixture in my house over the holidays. Whenever she wasn't at her daughter's house, she was here.

"That can't be true."

"Life is mysterious," I said. "I don't know why it's so, with the sauce. If I didn't know better, I'd say you deliberately left one little thing out so I'd never get it quite right."

She opened her mouth to answer, then shut it quickly when she realized I was joking.

"When do you have to move?" Michelle asked quietly.

"At the end of this month."

So she had a couple of weeks. "Well, I want you to think seriously about my offer, okay?"

She took my hand and pressed it briefly. "I promise you I will."

I looked at the two of them, sitting there. Michelle, my oldest and dearest friend. And Anna, a more recent friend, but just as precious to me.

"You know," I said, "I know that both of you are worried about staying here, but I have to tell you, I like the company. I had a big family back home, and some of the unhappiest times I've had in this house have been alone, eating a meal in my breakfast nook."

Something very subtle seemed to shift in Anna's expression. I knew Michelle realized I was kind of positioning her with Anna so the older woman would be more comfortable. Michelle and I have been in and out of each other's lives and homes since the first grade. We're as comfortable with each other as sisters—the good kind, the kind that want to be in each other's lives.

"Not that Ming and the cats aren't good company. They are. If I could just train the three of them to carry on a decent conversation, I'd be set. But I haven't quite gotten around to it yet."

Anna was shaking her head, her dark eyes amused.

"Michelle is staying here while her whole divorce is going down, but she'll be getting another job shortly as she always does, and if it's a movie that goes on location, I'll be back in the breakfast nook, talking to myself, babbling away. And soon I'll probably be so lonely that I'll start walking the streets and babbling, and they'll have to come and take me away—"

"All right, all right," Anna said. "I'll strongly consider the possibility! Is that all right with you?"

"Just one more thought," I said. "It would be much easier on me, not to mention the price of gas, if you lived here and made the sauce as opposed to making me drive all the way out to Riverside to fetch it."

"You really think my sauce is better?"

"I know it is. And since one of the subspecialties of my catering company is the excellent Italian food I've been making since I came home from Rome, your sauce would help me increase my business."

"Eva," Anna said, setting down her tea. "You are a dear, sweet girl with a generous heart. And I want you to know that I'll think about your wonderful offer carefully and let you know within a few days."

It was the way she had to do it, and I respected her.

"Great."

Michelle eyed Anna's hair. "As long as I've got my

scissors out, do you want me to give you a quick trim? Your bangs look a little shaggy."

"I would love it!"

I headed toward the kitchen and my workstation, wanting to run tomorrow's menu off so I could double-check that I had all the necessary ingredients. As I left them in the kitchen, I could hear Michelle saying, "Your hair is such a lovely silver, Anna, but I know of this great shampoo that would bring out the high-lights even more . . ."

I just read an article which said more people are de-pressed and medicated than ever before in America. And I wondered about this. Wouldn't you think that, given these statistics, we'd take a look at our culture and figure out that we might be doing something wrong?

I often thought about things like that when I cooked. I also believed that cooking and great food were central to a family's happiness. It seemed like nobody got to-gether for a home-cooked meal anymore. When I was a kid it was my favorite time of day, a time when we could discuss what had happened at school and kind of catch up with everyone else. But now everyone was too busy.

There were parts of the Italian lifestyle that I never gave up, even after coming back from Rome. My family background was Swedish and German, but I'd discovered part of my heart in Italy.

I remembered sitting at a café just off the Piazza Navona, at a little table in the sun, sipping a latte and thinking, *This is the life*.

I also remembered watching an older couple enjoying their coffee that same morning, and thinking, *America is no place to grow old*.

I couldn't stop thinking about Anna as I prepared for my Tuesday-morning catering job. This was an easy job, and one that I really enjoyed. A group of older women in Pasadena had hired me to cater their monthly reading group. It was a lot more fun than mine. All of these ladies were avid mystery readers, and they had the idea of going through the alphabet and reading all sorts of mysteries based on the author's last name.

On their second go-around of the alphabet, the Ladies Mystery Group were up to the letter K and I think this month the book was by Laurie R. King, something about a beekeeper. Some of the choices sounded so interesting as I was cleaning up—they always chose the next book at the end of the meeting—that I'd picked up a few. I'd really enjoyed *Good Night, Irene* by Carole Nelson Douglas. That was when they'd been back at the Ds.

This month they wanted my banana nut-crunch muffins, along with excellent coffee and an assortment of teas. The setup was easy compared to other catering jobs, and they were all really sweet ladies. So Tuesday morning promised to be a no-stress kind of job.

Anna called me as I was loading everything into my van.

"I need to talk to you, Eva."

"I'm on my way to a job." Inspiration struck. "Actually, I could use some help. Can I pick you up and we can talk on the way?"

"Of course. Do I need to wear something special? Black pants and a white shirt?"

"No, just come as you are. This group is pretty informal."

It worked out perfectly. I put Anna right with the muffins and she plated them up and talked to these ladies as if she was born to cater. I'd set up the urns with coffee and hot water, and placed tea bags, sugar, lemon and cream nearby.

There was always a huge lull while they discussed the book, and Anna and I managed to talk quietly as we cleaned up a little and packed away what we could. One of the things I did for this group was make extra muffins for the women to take home. I had a feeling some of these older ladies cooked just for themselves, and I knew what that was like. A muffin could be a snack that evening while watching television, or it could be part of breakfast the following morning.

As much as I love to cook, even I know that sometimes it's nice to have someone else do it for you.

So after Anna and I refilled the muffin trays and topped off the sugar and cream, we sat behind the tables and talked.

"Were you serious about my coming to live with you until I figured out what to do?" she whispered.

"Absolutely."

"And you weren't making up a story about my sauce?"

"No." This may sound strange, but I'm telling the truth about this one. Two people can make the exact recipe, and one batch comes out so much better than the other. I think it's partly when something is cooked with love, and it's partly the attention a cook gives to her work.

"So I could help you with your business?"

"Look at what you did today."

"I don't want to be a burden to you, Eva."

"I know."

"But I don't want to go to live at that place in Riverside. I feel like I would just be going out there to die."

"I agree completely."

"Tell me what else I could do for you."

"For starters, you could eat meals with me so that when Michelle goes on location, as I'm sure she will soon, I won't have to eat alone. You can keep the animals company when I have a late catering job, it helps them to have someone in the house. During the holidays, I've even hired a pet sitter to keep them company because I'm out of the house so much."

"I can do that."

"Things really pick up in May and June with all the weddings. February has a little bit of a crunch because of Valentine's Day. But if I could count on you to kind of oversee things at home, that'd be great."

"All right. And Eva, I won't get in the way of your meetings, I'll make a point of staying in my room—"

I wanted to throttle that daughter.

"No, I think we'd like your company. For starters, you can tell us how you made your marriage work for forty-five years."

"I don't know if I have a formula."

"You have to have some secrets."

"Just common sense."

"We could do with a little of that, things are so crazy these days."

"All right," she said. "When do you want me to move in?"

"What's good for you, Anna?"

"If I came right away, I could give my daughter back the money she loaned me this month."

"Then let's move you tomorrow. I have a neighbor with a truck—"

"I don't have any furniture, just two suitcases and a couple of little things."

Then I remembered. When her daughter had encouraged her to move out of the home she had shared with her husband, she'd sold most of her mother's possessions. It wasn't that I was hung up on having things, but I was sure a few pieces of furniture, a couple of knick-knacks, would have had comforting memories for her.

And I didn't even want to think about what had happened to the money from the sale of her house. A property bought in Southern California some time in the sixties and sold now, when prices were so high? How could Anna be short of funds? I had a feeling I knew the answer to that one.

Her downfall had been trusting people who should have been there for her, who should have loved and cared for her and seen to her welfare.

Well, as Ariel always said, we had to start from where we were. No looking back, because sometimes it could be just too damn painful.

"Two suitcases?"

She nodded her head, that head held high. Anna has perfect posture, no dowager's hump for her. She walked everywhere, and didn't seem to have any health problems except for a touch of depression. I thought it was situational, and who could blame her?

She was a proud woman, and I knew I had to tread carefully so as not to upset that pride.

"Why don't we just go get your stuff on the way home. Of course, you'll want Ming to sleep in your room with you tonight."

She nodded again, then glanced away, her attention supposedly fixed on the woman standing in front of the reading group, in the process of selecting the next book, a novel whose author's name began with L. But I'd seen the brightness of her eyes, the quick flare of hope. It had to be pure hell growing old when you had no family you could depend on.

Instinct told me we'd be just fine. And Ming would be happiest of all.

CHAPTER 8

When Anna and I arrived back at the house, Michelle had already left. She'd fastened a note to the fridge with a magnet telling me that she was on her way to Santa Monica and her shopping date with Ariel for the power suit. She'd left early and decided to do some errands on the way.

It worked out well. Anna and I had stopped at her retirement home after finishing up the mystery group and setting the date for the following month. This next time, with the L author, they'd decided to go with cookies and a cake. I liked these ladies, they always seemed to have so much fun at their group, and it was a good energy.

Anna didn't want any help packing, and she was done faster than I would've thought. Her movements were brief and economical as she packed every single thing she owned into two average-size suitcases and three boxes. That and her little television finished her packing. It took me only three trips to the van to carry all her stuff out, and one of the guys at the front desk helped me with her television.

Now we were back at the house, and I knew the room I had in mind for Anna. I hoped she'd like it.

"I don't want to go all Harry Potter on you, but there's this cute little room right below the stairs."

"I'm sure it will be fine."

It was a pretty large room, very cozy, with a slanted ceiling. I'd managed to fit in a double bed, a dresser and a wardrobe. I considered it one of the guest rooms, and now I could see that Anna would have even more space than she'd had at the home. Who knew what the arrangements would have been in Riverside.

"This is lovely," she said, setting down one of the lighter boxes on the bed.

"I think the dresser is empty," I said, quickly checking. The wardrobe only held a few blankets, and I left one at the foot of her new bed before taking the others upstairs.

By the time I returned with clean sheets and pillowcases, she had her television hooked up. Ming was perched on the bed, and her dresser drawers were open. She had one of the suitcases open and was transferring clothing to the drawers.

What could it be like, I wondered, to have everything you own in a couple of suitcases and a few boxes? What would that be like, toward the end of your life? It wasn't that I didn't think that most people had too much stuff. I read something somewhere that said that most families had an average of fifteen boxes in their garage or attic or basement that just kept coming with them every time they moved and were never sorted out.

They should do a reality show about that. Just switch boxes and let two different families unpack them and decide what to do with them.

But at the opposite end of those fifteen mystery boxes were Anna's two suitcases, her three boxes and her little thirteen-inch TV.

I knew a lot about her life. She'd told me about her marriage and two children. Her son lived on the East Coast. Anna's husband had died five years ago. She'd married him when she was twenty-one; he'd died in his sleep when she was sixty-six. She'd been by herself for the last five years. From everything she'd told me, the marriage had been a happy one.

How did you go on after your husband of forty-five years passed away? All that life, the vividness, the memories and the years had come down to a small room beneath the stairs, and a daughter who wanted to park her out in Riverside.

"Do you want to finish unpacking, or would you like to have some tea? I have a few of those muffins left."

"I'll join you in twenty minutes."

As I left her room I noticed that Riley, my younger cat, had poked his orange-and-white face around the door and was curiously surveying the scene. I had a feeling that Anna might have more than Ming for company tonight.

I went back to the kitchen and started washing up the serving trays. One of the reasons I'd bought this house was the enormous amount of cupboard and storage space, ideal for all the equipment a caterer needed. I dried the trays, put them away, and was just about finished cleaning out the huge coffee urn when Anna came into the kitchen.

Without missing a beat, I filled up the kettle and put it on the stove, then turned up the flame.

"Muffins are warming in the oven," I said. "I'll just be a minute."

Then the two of us carried it all out to the breakfast nook. I'd painted it a light yellow and the café curtains had a fruit-and-vine pattern. It's not like there isn't enough sunshine in Southern California. It's just that I like to see something cheerful first thing in the morning. Since I wasn't a morning person, I needed all the help I could get, and a cheerfully decorated nook seemed to be doing the trick, at least most days.

"Do you like the room?" I said as I poured boiling water over the tea bag I'd selected, a decaf black tea with natural vanilla flavoring. Anna had gone with her new favorite, lemon green tea.

"Yes. I do. It's close to the kitchen and the main bathroom, and that's perfect for me."

"So you wouldn't be crazy about doing stairs."

"I'd be all right with it, Eva. But I like where you put me just fine."

"All done unpacking?"

"Most of it. I might need a little help hanging up some pictures. If you don't want nails in the wall, I can put them on the dresser."

"Whatever you want is fine."

We sat in silence for a short while, enjoying the tea and muffins. I'd heated them up and put a little butter on the table. Not high tea, but very tasty all the same.

"This group," Anna said. "What's the purpose of it?"

"We all want to get married. We're sick of being single, but we hate to date."

"Hmm," she said, and took another sip of tea.

With many older women, you might have expected them to say, "Well, if you girls put half as much time into catching a husband as you did into your careers, you might get somewhere." Not Anna. It was one of the reasons I knew this decision to have her come live here for a while, until she figured out things with her daughter, had been the right one.

"It's harder now," she said. "To find a good man. I feel sorry for the women of today."

"In what way?" I replied. This was one of my favorite things, the whole period of winding down after a job. I never got tired of enjoying a cup of tea or coffee, some of the leftover food, and the time to relax.

I had some files on my computer, and usually I'd go right to it and type in what had gone right, what had gone wrong, ideas I had for the future, anything that would help me do a better job the next time.

But the Ladies Mystery Group was a no-brainer since they were very precise about what they wanted each month. So now I could just relax and take it easy, the calm before the storm. I still had the Wednesday-night breakup tomorrow night and then Thursday night at the art gallery, so it made sense to take some quiet time now, kind of pace myself.

It was almost as if the breakfast nook was my own little café. I swear I think that's why the French and Italians are less depressed than Americans are. We have our shrinks and our drugs; they have their cafés.

"I think you girls have less support. You have to do everything on your own. The culture isn't set up to help you at all. Not like it was when I was young."

"So you think you had more opportunities to meet people?"

"I think people were more social. They were less consumed with work. We had little get-togethers, like card parties, dinners, people came over for coffee and cake. It seemed slower somehow, the whole pace of life. Maybe it was just the times. We had a real neighborhood, where everyone knew each other. Now it seems much more impersonal."

"Give me an example."

"Oh, if you saw a man and you were attracted to him, someone on the block knew who he was or who he was related to. Knew his history. So you weren't always going out with complete strangers."

"That would be handy."

"But I think you girls are smart to set up this group and help each other. You need support in doing anything in life, especially finding the man you're going to spend the rest of your life with. Just promise me you'll try to find someone with a good character."

It had been a long time since I'd heard that phrase. Yeah, we'd come a long way, but the question was, had we moved in the right direction?

I filled her in about Wendy and her situation, and that she might be crashing at the house for a few days or even a couple of weeks.

"No matter how it broke her heart, she should have let this man go when she found out he was married and he'd lied to her," Anna said. "That's a huge deception, to lie every single day to someone who's been with you for several months. He was trying to get her trust while pretending to be something he was not."

Now, *this* was the kind of advice we needed. I couldn't agree more. But it seems as if when you're with your girl-friends, you can—or actually, *I* can—kind of sneak around the truth and find myself agreeing with them, letting them make excuses for their boyfriends.

Not Anna, though. She called it like she saw it—a man who lied to a woman for six months wasn't worth spending one more second with.

"I think she just got really attached to him."

"Of course she did, but no matter how much she hurt, she should have ended it right then. There's no future for her with this man, and I think deep inside she had to know it."

The thought had crossed my mind. I told Anna that the point of Wendy hiding out here was so her married boyfriend wouldn't be able to call her and talk her into giving him another chance like he had the other two times.

"That I understand. Sometimes it's easier to go with what we know than to strike out and try something totally different. I just hope Wendy doesn't start to believe that good things can no longer happen to her."

I told Anna about the way the group had begun.

"You have that kind of face, Eva, a face that inspires trust. And then, of course, you're one of the kindest people I know, so she knew she could confide in you."

"I'm glad we started the group up. I kind of felt like I was getting obsessed with work, and I didn't want to look back at my life and have it be nothing but work."

"Balance," Anna said softly. "And also having the wisdom to know when you're entering another time of life. When my Raymond died, I knew I was beginning another part of life, almost unbearable. But I had to face it. There had been so much we'd faced together, and all of a sudden I found myself alone."

"How did you get through it?" I couldn't imagine losing someone I'd loved for forty-five years.

"I woke up one morning and looked at the ceiling and I thought, 'Today is the day. Today is the day I have to decide if I'm going to live or die. And if I decide to die, then I have to get on with that, too.' But I decided to live. And it wasn't as if I put Raymond behind me. I feel as if he's always with me. But I knew I had to live for myself, I had to want to live, and embrace it. I couldn't just walk myself through the motions anymore."

"When did this happen?"

"About three months after he passed away. Those first few weeks were the most terrible of my life. I was lost, I felt like a child, crying inside all the time. But I just forced myself to go through my days. I tried to think of good things that were coming, and as time passed, I healed. But the most important thing was that I decided to be happy. I made that choice."

So simple, yet so hard.

"I don't know what's going to happen with Wendy."

"We'll keep her busy. I was thinking that if you didn't mind, I could do a little work with the plants around your house."

"Anna, I don't want you to think that you have to work nonstop to justify being here."

"No, I don't feel that way. I just love to work in the garden. Raymond and I used to grow the most delicious tomatoes and peppers. We had so much fun watching them come up, he used to tease me and call them his children. And oh, when we cooked them, the smell would fill the house."

Anna and I have that food link. The genetically altered, overprocessed food of today wasn't for either of us. Give me a tomato right off the vine in the summer, so juicy that when you bit into it the juice ran down the sides of your mouth. Give me a summer pasta sauce made with roughly chopped fresh tomatoes, some garlic, olive oil, basil and the best Parmesan Romano cheese. I must have been Italian in a past life.

"Thank you, Eva," Anna said, reaching for my hand. "Thank you for giving me this chance and letting me have a little more time. A little more time that's happy."

"My pleasure," I said. And I meant it.

Wednesday afternoon I spent so much time pawing through my closet wondering what to wear to the restaurant that Michelle finally came into my room, looked at the six outfits I had on the bed and ruthlessly picked one.

"A pantsuit? Flats?"

"In case we have to run. You'll notice I'm not wearing heels, either."

"Run from what?" I asked.

"I don't know. But it feels a little like we're being spies— I was just thinking, what would Charlie's Angels wear?"

I had a moment's flash of a brief bikini and a bright smile, but decided to go with the pantsuit.

We drove to Ariel's condo, taking Michelle's Volvo station wagon. She could pack a ton of stuff into it. When she did makeup for fashion shoots or head shots on location, she could practically set up a miniature makeup and hair salon.

She'd cleared it out today. One of the errands she'd done yesterday was to take her car to a car wash and had both the interior and exterior cleaned.

"A new beginning," she said as we pulled up at Ariel's condo. "You can always tell a woman's state of mind by the state of her car and her closet."

My van was always clean because it had to be. My closet was still something of a disaster. I wondered what that signified?

We sat in the car until we saw Ariel, in her BMW Roadster, come shooting down the street and into her building's driveway. Then we got out of the car, locked it and headed toward her front door.

Ariel always wanted to live near the beach, from the first moment she moved to Los Angeles from Texas. She was about a mile from the Pacific, and loved it. I'd fallen in love with Pasadena, which reminded me of a small Midwestern town, when I visited a friend who'd just bought a house there.

Ariel's condo was all sleek and modern and on the top floor, which in the case of this building was the fourth floor. She let us in the front door and we all took the elevator up.

We were right on time, but Ariel skidded to a stop, absolutely stunning in one of her new suits. She tossed her huge tote and what looked like an armload of manuscripts onto a chair in the hallway, then went down the hall to her bedroom.

"I'll be just a minute. Make yourselves comfortable."

I walked into the living room, which was also sleek and modern, and over to the windows. She had a view to die for—palm trees and clear blue skies.

When Ariel finally came out, both of us stared. She was wearing a red dress practically shrink-wrapped to her body.

"Don't say anything, I talked with Frances on the phone and we came up with a little plan in case Wendy falters."

"I don't even want to know—" I began, but the doorbell rang and Ariel ran to let Frances in. I heard Frances say, "It's perfect!" and wondered what the two of them had concocted.

"What?" I said when they came back into the living room. "Tell us what you're going to do."

"Well," said Ariel, "there's a darling jacket that goes with this dress, so it's not like I'll be going into the restaurant like this. I'll keep the jacket on unless Wendy decides she can't bring herself to break up with the jerk."

"And if she can't?" said Michelle.

"Then I take off the jacket and saunter by, and if he's as big a rat as I think he is, he'll go after the cheese."

I thought about this for a half second, then said, "Good plan. Why didn't I think of it?"

* * *

We all piled into Michelle's station wagon and drove to Wendy's place.

Or rather, Wendy's house. I'm sure that with the money she makes as a model, the house was something of an investment or a tax write-off. Still, when we found it in a very upscale section of Santa Monica, it took my breath away. It looked like the cutest little French château, tucked away behind some exquisite landscaping.

One of the things I loved about Southern California was how you could find Tudor next to stucco next to flat-out modern. In this case, the house resembled a tiny little castle with simple, elegant lines.

We walked up the driveway and rang the bell. The door was curved on top, and a beautiful solid oak. Everything seemed to fit, right down to the lush white flowers planted on the walkway. Anna would know their names, but I could never remember.

Wendy opened the door and she had on one of the most stunning dresses I'd ever seen. Short and sexy with just a little bit of sparkle. High heels, diamond earrings, subtle makeup. I hoped she'd thought to use waterproof mascara, and picked one that worked.

"Hey, come on in," she said, and we entered.

There were two things I noticed right from the start.

She was the sort of person who had traveled all over the world and picked up the most exquisite pieces, and she had family photos all over. But it didn't look cluttered or hurriedly thrown together. There were some green plants, mostly palms, and I saw a flash of ruddy fur as a cat came scampering over to investigate. An Abyssinian, and a gorgeous specimen.

"Say hi to Max," she said. "I just have to get my wrap."

Max was quite a well-mannered fellow, rubbing up against our legs but not using his claws on us. And I thought about how our pets reflect us in a funny way. Here was Max, exotic, just like his owner.

"Is he going to stay here alone?" I said.

"I left him lots of dry food and water, and I have a pet sitting service coming in twice a day to feed him and play with him."

"Excellent." I noticed she had a large bag with her as well as a small clutch. It looked like the sort of bag a person used for a weekend away. She caught me eyeing the bag and said, "So we can leave directly from the restaurant and not even come back here."

"Great idea."

The bag was thrown into the back of the station wagon, all five of us got in, Michelle and Wendy in front, and Wendy gave Michelle directions to the restaurant.

***

It was like entering another world.

When I was a child, eating out was a rare thing. First of all, my parents didn't have that much money when we were young. And second, they had four kids. There was Meg, then my older brother, Tim, then me and then my younger brother, Johnny. So the type of dining out that we were used to was the occasional— and I mean the *very* occasional—meal at a drive-in while my parents tried to get in some rest and relaxation. Stuff along the lines of chili dogs and fries and milk shakes.

Not that food has to be expensive to be good. If I learned one thing in Rome it was that simplicity, seasonal food prepared with loving care, always worked.

But the place we were walking into was beyond my wildest dreams.

I knew nothing about architecture, but this place was designed for comfort and relaxation. Italian marble. Tasteful, simple accents. We were shown to our table immediately, and I was sure the rest of the service would be at the same high standard.

Wendy had assured us that her waiter friend would pick an inconspicuous table and we were seated a little ways away from the main floor. The best part was that it had great concealment thanks to several large plants.

"I can't believe this," Frances whispered. "We're literally behind the potted palm!"

"Can you see her?" Ariel whispered back.

"There she is," I said, pointing but keeping my hands close to the table. "Don't everyone look at once!"

Of course they did. Thank God for potted palms.

For about a minute we were silent. Because this man, this married man had it all, the height, the build, the cheekbones, the facial symmetry, the eyes, the hands—

I got it. I got why she couldn't let him go once she found out he was married, and I got why she took him back twice. Men that rarefied came along once in a lifetime. But even looks like those couldn't justify such rotten behavior.

"He's movie-star handsome," whispered Michelle.

"What did she say he did?" Ariel asked.

"I can't remember," I said.

"Who cares?" said Frances.

"Okay, one of us has to let her know we're here," Ariel whispered. She beckoned a waiter over, then said with her sweetest smile, "Which way are the restrooms?"

Our luck seemed to be holding. To get to the restrooms, we'd have to walk straight past their table.

"I'll go," said Frances. She was dressed in a classic little black dress that looked wonderful with her newly colored hair. We watched her as she walked slowly past the table and Wendy saw her. Frances gave no indica-tion that she knew the two of them, simply continued on her way.

While she was gone, we were presented with menus—with no prices.

"This is how you know it's expensive," Ariel muttered.

"Please, let's not embarrass Wendy," I said. "Let's all try to look like we eat at places like this every night of the week."

"Boy, would that be fantastic," said Michelle.

"Not to mention hell on a diet," I said, frowning. As I scanned the menu, the foodie in me realized that this evening could give me some wonderful ideas for my catering company. After all, my subspecialty was Italian, and this was an Italian restaurant.

"Shall we all order something different and pass it around like at a Chinese restaurant?" Michelle sug-gested.

"Fine by me," Ariel said. "But we should wait until Frances gets back before we order."

"Somehow I suspect this isn't going to be the sort of place where they rush you," I said.

Frances came back to the table a moment later and slid into her seat. "He's even better looking up close!"

"When do I get to go to the ladies' room?" Ariel said.

"Not yet," I muttered, trying to peer through the palm fronds. "We can't let him get suspicious. Okay, you guys figure out what you want to order, and I'll keep an eye out for Wendy's signal. I already know what I'm going to order."

"Shrimp?" Michelle guessed.

I nodded my head, keeping an eye on Wendy and her married man. I turned my head just enough so it wouldn't look like I was staring.

"I'm thinking the portobello mushroom," said Michelle.

"That looked good," said Ariel.

"Both of you get it," Frances said. "I may go for this chicken dish, it looks fantastic. Or maybe the fish."

"How much money are we talking about here?" said Ariel. "What's our budgetary bottom line?"

Frances named a sum that almost made me fall out of my chair.

"We could get some wine with dinner!" said Ariel.

"One bottle between all of us," I said. "We have to have a clear head for this operation."

"What about dessert?" said Michelle.

"Ask if it can be served with the meal. We don't know when we'll have to ask for the check and make a run for it."

"Good idea." Michelle went back to scanning the menu.

I kept watching Wendy, and the entire time all I could think of was how heartbreakingly vulnerable she looked. And I couldn't understand how a woman as beautiful as she was could fall for a guy like this. Yes, he was a regular Adonis. But watching him, I could so clearly see the way he was looking at her. She was a conquest, nothing more, a notch in his proverbial belt. A little trophy to shout to the world that he still had it, that this was the sort of woman he could have.

Suddenly I didn't feel so hungry anymore. And of course at that exact moment, our waiter appeared.

"You're Wendy's friends?" he whispered.

"Yeah."

"Help her get away from this creep," he said, then, glancing over his shoulder and giving Wendy a quick look, he turned back to us and began to take our orders.

We got through our wine, appetizers and even the first part of our dinner before Frances said, "She's tugging on her earlobe and pushing back her chair. Okay, who's going in?"

"You and Eva," Ariel said instantly. "Michelle and I are the second string, so this guy doesn't get suspicious."

"Okay," Frances said, turning toward me. "Let's go."

CHAPTER 9

The bathroom was probably as spectacular as the rest of the place, but I barely gave it a glance. Both Frances and I homed in on Wendy, in a chair in the spacious sitting area before the sinks and stalls.

"What's up?" I said softly. This was still, after all, a public place, and I was sure she didn't want to call unnecessary attention to herself.

"I need a little bit of a push," Wendy admitted.

I could feel Frances's frustration. Well, a divorce did that to you. I jumped in before she could say or do anything.

"So what I'm understanding is that it's easy to do it in your head, or in your thoughts, but now that he's right here in front of you—"

"Yeah." She glanced away from both of us, and I could tell she was ashamed. But then I thought about the way she'd asked us to come to this Italian restaurant. There had been a reason, and this was it.

"What do *you* want, Wendy?" I asked gently. "Because we can support you, but we can't force you. And we sure don't want to do anything that would make you hate us afterward."

"I know I need to get him out of my life," she whispered, and I could tell she was trying very hard not to cry.

Breakups are just the worst.

In a rare moment of inspiration, I remembered part of what that breakup book had listed in one chapter about things to do to get over the guy.

"Quick," I said, knowing she couldn't stay in this bathroom with us all that long without her boyfriend getting suspicious. "Think back on a terrible memory you have of him. How about last Christmas Eve?" I knew I was hitting below the belt and going for the jugular, but there wasn't a married man I was aware of who got the holidays off. That was if his wife was smart and knew about his little games on the side, he didn't.

Wendy considered this for a moment and I said, "Where were you? What did you do? What did you eat? What were you thinking?"

"I was in Paris," she said slowly, and I thought, *Uh-oh…*

"I was in Paris, working for a magazine, and we were supposed to meet in London and spend Christmas Eve together, but he—he called at the last moment and said he couldn't get away from L.A., that something had come up with one of his daughters—"

Fantastic. This man has daughters and he treats women like this? It just gets worse and worse.

"You're right," Wendy said, looking first at me and then Frances. I swear her eyes looked clearer. "I'm not saying I may not need you all again this evening, but you've both given me the shot in the arm that I needed."

"Get out there and break up!" I said, giving her arm a squeeze. I swear to God I felt like a football coach in one of those rah-rah sports movies.

Wendy left and Frances and I fell down on two of the cushy chairs.

"I clutched," Frances said, her voice low. "All the anger I thought I was finished with, all the anger I had toward my ex came back and I just wanted to go out there and throttle the bastard."

"But you didn't," I pointed out. "Let's get back to dinner and keep an eye on her."

We returned to our table where Ariel and Michelle were anxious for news.

"What happened?" Ariel whispered, as if afraid the people near us might overhear.

"She had a moment of weakness and we talked her out of it," Frances said quietly.

"But we're not out of the woods," I warned. "Far from it."

"My stomach keeps churning," Michelle said.

"That could be from sampling everyone's dishes plus a tiramisu and those scoops of gelato—not that there's anything wrong with that." I almost laughed at the sight of us, all the plates spread out over our little round table. This whole evening was approaching the surreal.

"Red alert," Ariel whispered. "It looks like she's moving in for the kill."

We all looked at that point, confident that our friend the palm was covering us up as well as could be expected. Wendy was leaning in toward the guy, her expression intent. He didn't seem pleased, because he leaned back and began to shake his head.

"What a prick," Frances muttered.

"I'll second that," said Michelle, taking a spoon and reaching for a taste of my chocolate mousse.

"Why do we do this to ourselves?" Ariel said. "I just don't understand why we have to—*Oh my God!*"

I glanced back at Wendy's table and saw that the bastard had just pulled what looked suspiciously like a black velvet jeweler's case out of his suit pocket. And I might add that it was a very expensive Italian suit, so beautifully cut that even I, no fashionista, could appreciate it.

"He's giving her a *ring?*" Michelle whispered, stunned.

"*Please* don't tell me that he's the one married man

in the entire city of Los Angeles who's actually going to leave his wife and marry her!" Frances said.

"She's pulling on her earlobe," Ariel said. "Should Michelle and I go?"

"No," I said suddenly. "I think we're going to need you and that red dress of yours, Ariel. Michelle, finish that mousse and ask our waiter for the check. Frances, keep an eye on that bastard and report back to me when I come back to the table. I'm going in."

And I left our table and walked swiftly toward the ladies' room. For the first time in my life, I truly understood the expression *All's fair in love and war.*

Wendy was in the sitting area with a stunned expression on her face. I sat down on the chair beside her and took her hand. It was cold and so I rubbed it gently. This woman might actually be in shock.

"Hey," I said, wondering what the hell to do.

She turned toward me and I've never in my life seen a more emotionally destroyed expression. From her eyes to the way she held her head and her mouth so tightly, as if trying to hold in all the pain in the world.

"He gave me a ring," she said.

"We saw."

"Eva, this is so far from what I want."

"I know." I was beginning to get the picture.

"It's like—a mistress ring. It's like what he's really saying to me is, 'Here, you beautiful dumb piece of shit, take this ring and shut up.'"

I didn't try to dissuade her of the idea, or come up with some reason, some far-fetched story that could make him appear to be a nice guy. He was buying her off, plain and simple.

And I so wished Anna was here, with her wisdom and strength and life experience and common sense. Then I thought, maybe I could channel her.

"You deserve so much better, Wendy. A man who really loves you and who you can have a future with."

She nodded her head.

"I'll get everyone ready to go, we can help you get out of this."

"Is everyone finished?"

Trust Wendy that, in the middle of her personal heartbreak, she wanted to make sure we'd had dessert. I thought of Michelle, and the last of my mousse.

"Yeah. We're done."

"I'm going to do it. I'm going to let the whole mess go."

"Good girl. And can I ask you one thing?"

"Anything."

"If you falter, or if it looks like things aren't going your way, can we send in the big guns?"

She smiled, but it was a sad smile. "You can do anything you want, just make sure Michelle's ready to take off."

"You got it." I squeezed her hand. "Be brave, Wendy. This is a huge turning point in your life. If I were you, I'd end it cleanly. It'll hurt like hell for a while, but we're all here for you."

"Thanks. How much time do you think Michelle needs to get the car?"

"Give us fifteen minutes. Can you last that long?"

"I've lasted eight years, I think I can manage another fifteen minutes." She gave my hand a squeeze. "Thanks, Eva, for everything."

She headed out the door as I stared after her. *Eight years?* Holy crap, I thought. Sometimes a particular expression was perfect for an occasion, and this was one of those times. Holy crap.

But the clock was ticking.

I reached our table in record time.

"Check paid?"

"Yes," said Frances. "And we left an *excellent* tip."

"Great. Michelle, we need you to go get the car and hover outside. And make sure the front seat stays empty for Ariel. Turn the car around so she can get right in, so it's facing the front of the restaurant."

"You got it." She stood up and went toward the exit and valet parking.

"Our boy's getting irritated," said Frances. "I think he's pissed that for once he's not getting his way."

"Too bad."

We watched them for another ten minutes, then I said, "Ariel, we need your red dress right about now. And if Wendy takes off, we'll have to rendezvous outside, where Michelle will have the car. You've got the front-passenger seat, and of course we'll wait for you."

"You guys'll be right out front? 'Cause I don't want to set off this bomb unless I can make a quick getaway."

"You will."

"Got it." She handed the jacket to me and stood up, smoothing the silky red material down over her thighs. She looked spectacular as she sauntered away from our table, directly toward Wendy and the rat in the Italian suit.

"And now it's time for us to get out," I said to Frances.

"Can't we just watch?" she said.

"Okay, but stand up and get ready to roll."

We stood, keeping our eye on Ariel, who was moving slowly, with great purpose, toward Wendy's table. Every man who saw her couldn't look away, the dress was that great and Ariel was working it for all she was worth.

"Any second now," Frances said, and I thought she

might have been talking about a detonation in one of those classic World War II movies as she whispered, "Closer, closer..."

And then Ariel scored a hit. Direct contact. Married Guy had been doing his best imitation of Sincere Fellow when his eye caught sight of her butt in that red dress. He stopped right in midsentence, literally couldn't stop looking, and we saw that Wendy got it.

She wrenched her hand out of his and pushed her chair away from the table, stood up and stormed toward the exit.

"And now," I said to Frances, "it's time to get out of Dodge."

We found the car in record time. Wendy was already inside, in the backseat with her head down. Michelle had given her a lap robe to put over her, and as we all watched, Ariel came racing out and dived for the front seat.

"Go, go, *go!*" she said, keeping her head down, and Michelle took off. Frances and I both looked back and saw Married Guy come running out to the sidewalk, pissed as hell that he couldn't figure out where Ariel had gone. Within seconds we turned the corner and were out of sight.

And within a few more seconds, Wendy's cell phone rang.

"Take it," she said, her voice muffled beneath the lap robe. She was still hunched over, the robe over her head, clearly in pain. I took her clutch and dug inside for her cell phone, then turned the ringer off and set it to vibrate.

Total silence in the car as Michelle drove smoothly through the evening streets. I handed Ariel the red jacket to her dress and she shrugged into it and buttoned it up.

"Thanks, you guys," said Wendy, and she sat up. The lap robe was now around her like a shawl, and I thought she had to be freezing in that dress.

"You forgot your wrap," said Frances.

"Greg will get it for me," she said, and I assumed she meant her waiter friend. I realized we'd been so nervous about the whole thing, we'd never introduced ourselves. But I had a feeling we'd be seeing more of him.

"Now where?" said Michelle.

"Home for me," said Ariel. "I have to be at work early tomorrow." She glanced into the backseat. "No hard feelings, Wendy? For what I did?"

"No," she said quietly. "You were great. What you did finally opened my eyes to who he really was. The worst-case scenario I could think of was that I would've wasted a few more years on him and he would've eventually dumped me for somebody younger."

I looked at Frances and Ariel with new respect. They'd come up with something pretty powerful. The four of us made a good team. Between all of us, we'd managed to break Wendy out.

Now I was using jail metaphors instead of my usual war ones.

We dropped both Ariel and Frances off at Ariel's condo. Frances walked off toward her car after assuring Wendy she'd call her in the morning.

"Hang tough," she said before she walked off. "The worst is over. You don't ever have to see him again."

"I don't want to," Wendy replied.

Then Michelle and Wendy and I were on the road, heading south on Lincoln before turning left onto the 10 East. It would take us straight to the 110 and right into Pasadena. We'd be home shortly.

Michelle drove calmly and quietly, without bothering to make any conversation. I think she thought, like I did, that the next step was to get Wendy home. I don't think either of us were thinking that far ahead, just taking things step by step.

"Keep my cell phone, Eva."

"Okay." I slipped it into my purse.

"Erase every one of his messages. Just let me know about any agency calls, and I'll call them back on your phone. I'll pay you for any charges."

"Sure."

"But keep it with you, and no matter what I say, don't give it to me."

I was pretty good with electronic devices, computers and phones and would have her phone figured out in no time. Michelle had offered her room upstairs for Wendy, saying she could either bunk in with me or sleep on the couch. I had a feeling we'd be up talking for a while, as neither of us had to work tomorrow. Just the gallery opening with Frances, and that was in the evening.

Harsh white lights overhead swooped in and out of the darkened car. Michelle was alone in the front seat, Wendy and I in the back. There was really nothing to say. I had a sense that Wendy actually needed the quiet time to assimilate all that had finally happened.

And as I watched the play of light over Wendy's profile, it struck me that so many women had such a narrow outlook on truly beautiful women. They could be hurt just as badly as anyone. Sometimes worse.

Mr. Married Man had thought that because Wendy was a model, she had to be dumb as a box of rocks. It had been convenient for him to think that way. He must have promised her the moon and she must have desperately needed to believe him to stick with him for eight years of her life.

Eight wasted years. The reality of that would hit her in the next few days, if not the next few hours.

I had a feeling it was going to be a long night.

* * *

When we walked into the house the kitchen lights were on, and once we got there, I saw that Anna was making tea. She had on a comfy red flannel robe and warm slippers. She smiled as we came into the kitchen, but her gaze went directly to Wendy.

Introductions were in order, so I said, "Anna, this is Wendy, Wendy this is Anna—" just as Anna said, "Oh, you poor thing," and held out her arms to Wendy. And Wendy just lost it, started to sob.

It was a testament to Anna's warmth that Wendy was about five foot eleven, and Anna only five-one, but the shorter, older woman enveloped the younger woman in a fierce hug and steered her toward the table in the breakfast nook.

Tea. We needed tea. Wasn't tea considered a cure-all for everything in England? And how could it hurt?

"What else?" Michelle whispered, and I swear it was like she could read my mind.

"I've got cinnamon rolls in the freezer, they won't take long."

So Michelle filled the kettle fuller and brought all the cups and spoons and tea bags and all the other stuff to the table. I slammed some cinnamon rolls on a cookie sheet and threw them into the oven, then took the timer with me and went into the breakfast nook. But before I did, I checked Wendy's cell phone.

Five messages, all from the same number. Oh, he was pissed all right. Pissed that eight years of convenience for him but eight years of heartache for her had come to an end tonight.

The cell phone vibrated in my hand once again, and I thought of the supremely spoiled man I'd seen tonight, his future thwarted.

Tough.

I ran up the stairs and put Wendy's cell phone in my bottom dresser drawer, tucked between my sweaters. No one had to worry about the phone for tonight. It could vibrate all it wanted among my sweaters.

Anna was in the breakfast nook with Wendy, Ming snoozing in her lap, listening to Wendy's entire story as if she hadn't just heard most of it from me less than thirty-six hours ago.

She didn't say a word, didn't ask for clarification. She just listened. And as she listened, I set the kettle on a trivet on the table and she fixed Wendy a large mug of lemon herbal tea with just a little honey in it, then pressed it into her shaking hands.

"Drink this," she said calmly. "It will help."

And Wendy did. When the cinnamon rolls reached the table, Anna took one and put it on a plate, then passed it to Wendy.

"I can't. My stomach—"

"Just a little piece, it will settle your stomach."

Wendy started to eat. As she ate the cinnamon roll and drank her tea, she talked and talked and talked.

Anna thought that I had a face that encouraged people to tell me things? But she was the Jedi Master of all listeners. By the time another hour had passed, Michelle and I—and Anna, of course—knew almost every single detail of her eight-year affair with Rick. Rick the prick. Sorry, it just flew into my head the minute I heard his name, and I will never think of him by any other name but that one.

It was as if she had to get it all out, spewing poison that had been steadily seeping through her bloodstream and infecting her body. We listened, all wound up from our night out, none of us ready for bed. And when Wendy finally yawned and Anna suggested that she try to get some sleep, Michelle took Wendy upstairs and showed her to her bedroom.

Anna and I made short work of the cleanup.

"She must never see this man again," Anna said as we left the kitchen. Ming had crashed; the black Pekingese was asleep in her arms, snoring softly through his flat little nose. "And she may be here longer than a week."

"I don't mind."

"She's a little lost soul, that one."

As I climbed the stairs to my room, I thought that Anna had summed it up perfectly.

* * *

I stayed up talking with Michelle about the whole evening.

"I can't believe how good looking he was," she said. "Even I would have had a hard time cutting that guy loose."

"But eight years?"

"I'd like to think that I would've ended it sooner, but look at me and Bryan. Now I'm beginning to wonder if he was ever faithful to me throughout most of the marriage. Maybe his twentysomething isn't the first."

Something had shifted in Michelle. It was almost as if she'd finished all her crying, was just done with it. I wondered about this, and thought that maybe she'd realized her marriage was over a few years before Bryan had been caught in the affair. Maybe the affair had simply been the catalyst that had set everything in motion.

"Where are those men we used to fantasize about in high school?" Michelle said. "Do you think they even exist?"

"I don't know. I think there are good men out there, but maybe we're as shallow as a lot of men are. I mean, look at Rick. We were all practically drooling when we saw him. But he really put her through hell, the self-centered bastard."

"Yeah, I guess—"

We both jumped as a sound started up from the depths of my dresser.

"Oh God, it's the phone!" I opened the drawer and got Wendy's cell phone out of my sweater drawer. The damn thing had been vibrating so much that it had worked its way out from between the sweaters and had fallen against the wood. Hence the noise.

"How many messages now?" said Michelle.

"Eleven."

"Erase them."

"I have to listen to them first—"

"Eva!"

"I do. I'm serious, Michelle. What if one of them is a family emergency?"

"If all the numbers are the same, it's him."

"I'm still going to listen—I want to know what she's up against."

"Well then, don't erase them, I want to hear, too."

So we listened, and heard how Rick was first cajoling, then mournful, then pleading. But by message number eleven, he was bordering on abusive. This man was clearly used to things going his way.

I erased all the messages after Michelle and I had listened to them, then buried her cell phone in a plastic crate filled with yarn in the back of my closet.

"No one can hear it there, and I can check it every couple of hours."

Michelle yawned and stretched out on the air mattress I'd set to the side of my bed. "I can't believe we have that gallery opening tomorrow night. It'll almost seem anticlimactic after what happened this evening." She paused for a moment, then said, "That sounded terrible and I know it. I shouldn't be talking this way about what Wendy went through tonight."

"No, it's okay, I know what you mean. I think we have to be pretty gentle with her tomorrow. I don't think she'll be in any shape to go to the gallery."

"Eva, don't you dare stay home! It's my goal in life to get you out of this house."

I smiled as I lay down in bed and closed my eyes. "I think we'll both be able to go. Didn't you see how she and Anna got along? I don't think we really have anything to worry about."

I turned off the light and we lay quietly in the darkness.

"Where are the cats?" Michelle whispered after a few minutes.

"Bongo and Riley have defected to Anna's room. She has an old-fashioned hot-water bottle, and both cats have decided it's their new best friend."

"Traitors!"

Another short silence, then Michelle said, "Do you think we'd make good spies?"

"I don't know about spies, but you'd make a hell of a getaway driver!"

I could hear Michelle turning in her bed, trying to get comfortable.

"Is that air mattress horrible?"

"No, it's actually quite comfortable. Do you think she'll end up going back with that guy?"

"Not if the look I saw on her face in the restaurant bathroom was anything to go by."

"That bad, huh?"

"Yeah. I don't ever want to feel that bad over a man."

"Speaking of feeling that bad over a man," Michelle said. "Do you think Frances would be able to steer me toward a great divorce lawyer?"

"That's a fantastic idea! We can ask her tomorrow at the gallery."

"I think I'm going to get through this, Eva. And it helps, being here, because between you and me and Anna and Wendy, it's like our own little sorority. Kind of a house filled with broken women."

"Speak for yourself," I said, then I buried my face in my pillow because I couldn't help laughing.

CHAPTER 10

Why had it taken five people—me, Ariel, Michelle, Frances and Greg the waiter—to help Wendy break up with Married Man? Who knew?

Personally, I couldn't imagine wasting eight years of my life on a man like that, especially if I looked like Wendy. But the whole experience taught me that it doesn't matter what a woman looks like on the outside, it matters what she feels like inside. And Wendy clearly thought she didn't deserve much more than this man.

The actual breakup of the relationship took place in an evening, in the course of a few courageous minutes. Wendy's rebuilding of her life was going to take a lot longer, and require a lot more bravery. If she was smart about it, she'd take some time to figure out why she stayed so long with a married man. What was going on there? That would be the hard part, the part she had to dig for, excavate, expose, and make sure she understood so she'd never repeat it.

We all did crazy things. There wasn't a woman on the

planet that hasn't made a bad choice when it came to a man. Some of those choices ended up getting women hurt or killed. But this whole relationship dance could really wound you. And that was where Wendy was right now.

I thought of all this the following night while at the art gallery on Melrose with Frances, Ariel and Michelle. Wendy had insisted that we still attend, she'd told us she was fine. But the thing that clinched the deal concerning leaving her at my home was that Anna was there—Anna the rock, with Ming the amazing Velcro dog. I knew Wendy was in good hands, so now it was time for me to launch myself into the wide world of dating.

I really didn't feel I had a choice as far as whether or not I was going to attend. I knew better than to try to talk myself out of it with Ariel, Frances and especially Michelle making sure I got out there and socialized. It was kind of like a Weight Watchers meeting—I knew I would be held accountable this coming Sunday, so I had to have something to report.

If I was truly honest with myself, I wanted to get out there and try to find a terrific man. I'd been alone too long, with all the food I cooked and with all my activities that revolved around women. I needed a good, stiff shot of testosterone in my life to liven things up.

As I scanned the enormous gallery, the high white walls filled with art, I was picturing those images from the beginning of *Terminator II*, that intricate computer program in Arnold's head that looked at people and sized them up immediately. While the Terminator had been looking for a decent set of clothing to cover up that amazing bod, *I* was merely looking for a man to flirt with, and perhaps exchange phone numbers for an exciting rendezvous in the near future.

It would make a very nice change.

That was the goal. Flirt and give out your phone number once you were asked. Line up potential dates for that once-a-week assignment. How hard could it be?

Well. The first three guys I felt absolutely nothing for, but the man I was talking with now definitely had potential. Nicely dressed, clean, seemed intelligent. He could talk about the art, which was largely modern and abstract, so I was out of my element. I just let him tell me what was going on in all those canvases. Or what he thought was going on.

This man standing directly in front of me, champagne flute in hand, talking about streaks of color and splatters of paint, had potential. *Great* potential. Sandy-blond hair, direct gray eyes, taller than I was and a good build. He was also easygoing and charming, and I could see myself having a really good time with him, though not necessarily heading to the bedroom unless I really got to know him better.

But there was that thing between us, that little "click." That spark of attraction. You knew it when you felt it, there was no way to fake it. Since I'd anticipated meeting dozens of men and not feeling that little click at all, this was an extremely pleasant surprise. I found myself really wanting to see where this could lead.

Austin. That was his name. I had immediately thought of that great city in Texas, with all the film festivals. Ariel had attended one of them with her screenwriting buddies. I had to do that, play with word associations, because I was so bad with names.

And Michelle was right, damn it. I *did* feel a lot more confident with my newly highlighted hair, a great new outfit she'd helped me find and killer shoes. I actually kind of tossed my head as he talked to me, then smiled up at him. He'd looked at my breasts a few times, but not enough to annoy me.

Anyway, if he asked me for my number and we went out a few times, there would be plenty of time to scope out whether or not he was a keeper. But the vibes I was getting right now told me that he liked me, and I thought he was worth giving my number to. I had the feeling he was going to ask for it.

Until…

"Austin? Why did you walk off and leave me with that woman?" A tall, very thin brunette came stalking up to us. She had to be almost six feet tall, dressed completely in black, with a closely cropped head of dark hair, a flat chest and barely any makeup. At first glance, I swear I thought she was a man.

"Hey, Cath," he said easily, and I tried not to show any reaction as she reached his side, threaded her arm possessively through his and glared at me.

Okay. So I had flirted with him. Tossed my newly highlighted head. We'd had a few laughs, talked art, had some champagne. He'd covertly glanced at my boobs. But I hadn't known he was *with* someone.

How nice of him not to mention her within the first five minutes of our conversation. How amazing men were, leaving out those little details. I thought of Wendy's Married Man. Typical.

"Hi, Cath," I said, trying to cover for Austin's insensitivity. I smiled and held out my hand. She continued to glare at me, then looked over at him, clearly ticked off. Suddenly he didn't seem so cute. My private attraction meter was doing a real nosedive.

If we'd just been talking, that would've been one thing. Cath would have to be truly neurotic to object. This was, after all, a public place. But he'd been into flirting with me, way deep. I wasn't being delusional about this. And I'd have been pissed too if he were my boyfriend.

She ignored my outstretched hand, and I remembered Ariel's little pep talk on the way to the gallery.

Just try to meet as many people as possible. Really get out there and mingle…

Somehow, I didn't think this was what she had in mind.

I was on my fourth flute of very good champagne, trying to get up the nerve to approach another group of people, when I spotted Michelle across the crowded gallery and practically did a spit take.

Was that who I thought it was? I could feel the vibe in the air, the way people were collecting, gathering around this man and Michelle. The air seemed to hum, practically vibrate.

This man. Try John *Dempsey.* Try a movie star the likes of Tom Cruise, George Clooney, Johnny Depp and Brad Pitt rolled up into one irresistibly hunky package. And here was Michelle, talking to him like she'd known him all her life.

I frowned. Maybe she had. Not known him all her life, because I would've remembered if a man like Dempsey had been in our high-school class. Even I hadn't been that much of a slacker. But Michelle worked with actors of his stature on movie sets all the time, so it wasn't unreasonable to assume she knew him. Perhaps he'd just stopped in to admire the art, and they'd struck up a conversation.

Los Angeles is such a small town. Spend any time at all in the City of Angels and you'll find out how true that is.

I decided to make my way over there. John Dempsey looked a lot better than any other man in the room.

"Hey," I said, walking up to the two of them.

"Eva!" Michelle said. "Just the person I wanted to see. John, this is my best friend in the entire world, Eva."

I literally almost passed out when he took my hand and shook it. The perfect handshake, just the right amount of pressure, and his hand was warm, not damp. The perfect light cologne, or his scent, or whatever. The perfect thick dark hair, dark blue eyes, chiseled cheekbones, facial symmetry, a full mouth that would make angels weep, and he was actually smiling down at me...

You get the picture. And when you blow that face up to fit a movie screen, this man was worth every bit of the millions of dollars that they paid him. No one, and I mean *no one*, could get both males and females in movie-theater seats on an opening weekend like John Dempsey.

Here he was, in the flesh. And here I was, mortified,

thinking of the vast sexual wasteland my life had been recently, and about the fact that sometimes, when I'd help myself along during these bleak times—I mean, literally give myself a hand—I would fantasize about Dempsey to make sure I achieved the desired outcome—the big O.

It was exactly like Carrie said in *Sex and the City*, about George Clooney being the gold standard, the Chanel suit of men we use in our sexual fantasies.

If Clooney was a classic Chanel suit that never went out of style, then John Dempsey with his well-worn blue jeans, scuffed black biker boots and black leather jacket with a classic white T-shirt was the definitive on-screen bad boy with a heart of gold. That rakish smile told a woman she'd have a good time and that he'd take care of her. Bad boys always had turned me on.

Thank God he didn't have a clue about what was running through my mind.

"You're the caterer, right?" he said.

So he listened, as well. I was such a sucker for a man who remembered details, and Michelle had obviously given him some.

"John's here to buy some art, isn't that exciting?" Michelle said.

I heard some garbled words coming out of my mouth, then I rallied. I cleared my throat and said, "So, you like this stuff?" Maybe that was what was wrong with him. Something had to be wrong with him; I had to find something wrong with him. That was it, maybe he had incredibly bad taste in art.

Those eyes filled with mischief as he looked down at the two of us. "Nope. Can't stand the stuff. A buddy of mine collects this guy's work, he couldn't make it, so I told him I'd show up and buy him a painting or two. Would you two help me out?"

"I can't stand modern art," I said, my voice low, and I swear to God, he threw back his head and laughed, then said, "Neither can Mick, so I'm out of luck."

Mick? Oh, *Michelle*. And as I glanced between the two of them, my intuition told me that something was definitely going on here. Dempsey had given her a nickname? Just how many films *had* they done together?

"Okay, I've got to get going on this before they're all sold," he said, and that killer smile literally had me weak in the knees. Austin who?

"What are you going to do?" Michelle said.

He looked at her and said, "Quick, don't think, pick a number between one and thirty-seven."

I almost choked on my champagne when I realized what he was up to.

"Seventeen," Michelle said.

Dempsey glanced at me. "Eva?"

"Thirty-two," I replied.

He marked his catalog in two places and said, "I'll be right back." Then he wove through the crowd toward the woman in charge of this whole thing.

Clever man. There were exactly thirty-seven paintings in this exhibit, and he'd got numbers for two of them. I had to admit I liked his style. Even though, to my mind, these paintings were outrageously overpriced, it obviously wouldn't be a problem for Dempsey, or his buddy.

I grabbed Michelle's arm and dragged her into a corner. "You never told me you *knew* him!"

"I've worked on three movies with him, Eva. He's a blast."

I knew there was something else going on, but now was not the time to ask.

"He's leaving for some location shoot in Hawaii in about two weeks, and he told me he was going to recommend me for a job."

Uh-huh. Forget not the time to ask, there *was* no time. "Micki, has he ever come on to you?"

"Once, the first movie we did together—the very first day, when I did his makeup. Until he found out I was married. Then he backed off."

Fantastic—looks like that and he had some morals. I glanced down and noticed that Michelle was still wearing her wedding ring, but decided not to say anything. If she wasn't ready, she wasn't ready. And really, it was only January and she'd just found out about Bryan's bimbo on the side on Christmas Eve. Perfect timing, ho ho ho.

We talked for a few minutes, comparing notes, and Michelle empathized with me that I still hadn't had one man ask for my number.

"No one in our dating club is going to blame you, Eva. The important thing is that you got dressed up, showed up and did your best."

I sighed. "Yeah, I know. Though I think Austin might have asked for my number if Cath hadn't dragged him away."

"You're better off without that loser," Michelle muttered, then glanced up. I saw that her gaze was on John Dempsey as he made his way through the crowd toward us. There was something in her eyes…

I just know her too well. I'm telling you, there was definitely something going on.

"Thank you, ladies. Two paintings bought for my buddy. They're going to deliver them over the weekend."

"Glad we could be of service," I said, glancing at Michelle. "You know, we should hire ourselves out."

"I bet you could," he said with that smile. So great,

just standing there, just watching him. And I so knew that he was so Michelle's, whether she knew it or not. My intuition, on red alert for my best buddy.

"Michelle tells me you're heading to Hawaii," I said, trying to slow my heartbeat down. If I thought this man did it for me on-screen or in my most private fantasies, that was nothing compared to Dempsey in the flesh.

"Yeah, it should be a good time."

I had the distinct feeling that this was a man who would have a good time no matter what he was up to. He'd make his own good time.

"What kind of movie?" I said.

"Action adventure."

What I loved about John Dempsey was that he made one huge blockbuster for every two or three little independent films. He'd even produced a few independents himself. He seemed a man at ease with himself, who had accepted the way the system worked and had found his place in it. You never heard him complaining about anything.

The press didn't seem to hound him the way they did other stars—not that they didn't want to. A picture of him could bring in a nice check. But from what I'd read, he lived a relatively private life and had made it difficult for them. You never saw him caught up in the scandals that other celebrities were prey to. He wasn't into crashing cars or partying the night away, let alone being one of the stars in an amateur sex video.

"I'm going to get Michelle out there, too," John said. "Two months on Kauai doesn't sound too bad, does it?"

Let me see, I thought. *One tropical paradise coming right up + this guy a stone's throw away—and probably shirtless—for weeks at a time = perfect divorce therapy.*

The only thing that could make it any better would be a full-blown affair...

Somehow, my daydreams or plans always had a wrench thrown into them, and this time was no exception.

I was still deep in my private fantasy, somewhere in the sand by a secluded lagoon on Kauai having a macadamia nut plucked out of my belly button by a man's sensuous lips when I heard Dempsey say, "So, how's Bryan doing?"

Then I heard Michelle say, "Just fine. Thanks for asking, John."

I almost did another spit take, wasting yet more of the fine champagne, then looked over at my friend. We communicated so well because we've been friends for so long, and her expression was clearly telling me, *Don't say anything, I'll explain later...*

Now I definitely knew something was up. And yes, she would explain later, in excruciating detail. But I'd have to catch her when the time was right. Sometimes Michelle can shut herself up tight as a clam and reveal absolutely nothing.

"Terrific meeting you," I said to John, shaking his hand one more time. "I've got some friends I need to meet up with, so I'll say goodbye."

His smile was easy and genuine. "I've heard a lot of good things about you, Eva. It was great to finally meet you."

I could sense the other women's envious eyes on me as I took my leave. As I walked away, I felt as if I were floating.

Not a bad evening, all things considered. I didn't even care that I'd walked away without a single dating prospect.

I'd met John Dempsey.

I took a break from the gallery opening and walked outside onto Melrose Avenue. On a Thursday evening the street wasn't all that crowded, but there was still plenty of action.

I opened my purse and pulled out Wendy's cell phone, deciding to get rid of the new bunch of messages. I listened to another six messages from Mr. Married, Rick the prick, then erased them. And then I called home.

Anna answered.

"How's everything?"

"Fine. Are you enjoying your evening?"

"So-so. No prospects yet."

"Don't get discouraged, Eva."

"I'm not. How's Wendy?"

"She's taking a hot bath, then we're going to watch a DVD."

"Excellent. Michelle and I shouldn't be more than a couple of hours. There's a blueberry cheesecake in the fridge if you want some."

"You didn't make it for a job?"

"Nope. I was testing a recipe, and it worked. Have at it."

We said our goodbyes, and I was about to put the phone back in my purse when it rang again. I instantly recognized the number. I mean, the guy had called so many times that it was practically burned onto my retinas.

Some little devil made me answer.

"Hel-*lo*," I said brightly.

"Wendy! You finally answered! Listen, you—"

"I'm sorry, I'm not Wendy."

"Huh?" And with that, he rattled off her number and asked me if he'd dialed the number incorrectly.

"No, you didn't. Who am I speaking to?"

"How did you get this phone?" He didn't sound

happy, and he didn't answer my question. Oh, the cheating married man, always covering his tracks. What a complete scumbag.

Now I knew exactly what I was going to do. I mean, how many times did this guy have to call before he got the message? And how many messages can one cell phone hold? Mr. Married had to be taught a lesson.

I have never been a really spiteful woman. I remembered hearing a story on *The View* about a woman who'd asked her boyfriend over for some after-the-breakup sex. While he was asleep, she'd super-glued his penis to his stomach, his testicles to each leg, and his butt cheeks together. When he'd woken up, she'd kicked him out of her house and he had to walk two miles to the nearest phone and call an ambulance to take him to the emergency room.

You never saw stories like that on *ER*. The ratings—especially male viewers—would plummet.

Anyway, in my opinion that was way out of line no matter what the guy did. But the little bit of mischief I was contemplating was nothing compared to the grief this man had caused Wendy for eight years. I wasn't saying she didn't play her part in the whole thing, because she let him get away with it. I just thought it was about time that Mr. Married was inconvenienced.

"Wendy gave me this phone and said she never

wanted it back. That was just before she left for the Bahamas."

"The Bahamas!"

"Yeah. Some sort of photo shoot or something, she has the most incredible job, and that photographer she was with was *so* cute—"

"Did she say where she was staying?"

"That new hotel, the Atlantis something? I think it was on Oprah."

"I know the one. Thank you, you've been very helpful."

You betcha.

He clicked off and I tucked the cell phone back in my evening bag. Well, that took care of Mr. Married. He'd be having a little fun in the sun before he realized Wendy was nowhere on the island.

Sometimes I amazed even myself.

On Friday night we decided that it was time for Wendy's official pajama pity party. So all of us brought our CDs with our saddest breakup songs, and our pj's and thick socks. In an inspired burst of creativity, I made an enormous bowl of chocolate-chip cookie dough. Frances brought salty snacks, pretzels and chips, and Ariel supplied the wine. I made sure we had several boxes of tissue for the romantic and tragic DVDs we'd be watching.

Anna had decided not to join in, but she'd bought Wendy a gift. When she opened it, right before we started the first DVD, all of us were impressed and quite moved by the lovely journal. Inside the front cover, Anna had written, "Sometimes it helps to write your most painful feelings down. That way they don't stay inside you."

Wendy had tucked the large blank book by her side, obviously touched. And I reached for the first DVD, Cary Grant and Deborah Kerr in *An Affair to Remember*.

"It's no coincidence that this movie was referenced during *Sleepless in Seattle*," I said as I set up the first DVD. "It's one of the great romances of all time, a real weepie."

"Yeah, yeah, where's *my* Cary Grant?" grumbled Ariel. Two guys had taken her number at the gallery opening, and neither had called yet, so she was grumpy. I thought she was being a bit hard on them, wanting a call within twenty-four hours. I think men had to think before they called, or something like that. Maybe it just took time for them to get their nerve up.

But if a week went by, then I'd consider both of them history.

"You might just be finding Cary tomorrow morning, at your screenplay group," Michelle said.

Ariel had decided to spend the night, and Michelle was going to help her get ready for her writing group the following morning. The big test, the power suit and fabulous makeup, to see if she could get these men—especially Nate—to regard her as more than the group's unofficial mascot.

The movie began, and we all settled back to watch.

A pity party was a very specific type of event. This was the only one I have ever catered, but the snacks were generally simple and straightforward. No one could bring in their complaints; the party had to center around the one person. In this case, that person was Wendy.

The ground rules were simple. This was an evening made for wallowing, for self-pity, for endless discussions about what had gone wrong and if-onlys. It was a noble attempt to get it all out of your system so you could start fresh. You could tell the same story twenty times at your own personal pity party. In fact, it was encouraged. If you told it enough, it started to lose its power.

The credits rolled, the music played. Various snacks were passed around, and we all settled back into chairs and on pillows, watching the television screen. Riley, a complete feline pretzel fiend, was perched on the back of Frances's chair, as near to the bowl as he could get without disgracing himself. It made a cute picture, as they both had dark red hair.

Bongo was snuggled in my lap.

I hadn't told Wendy about Married Man's impromptu

trip to the Bahamas. He'd certainly be there by now. Her cell phone was set on vibrate and hidden way back in my upstairs closet among the yarn.

She'd given me permission to talk to him, to do "whatever I felt was best." It almost gave me more pleasure than the movie to think of him racing around the island trying to find Wendy. Kind of a demented affair to remember.

Maybe next time he would think twice before lying to someone who cared for him. Whatever discomfort this little trip created for him, it sure beat being super-glued.

CHAPTER 11

The following morning Ariel left for her writing group looking like an absolute knockout. Michelle had done her hair and makeup, then went back to bed. She'd been up late last night, talking with Wendy. I'd fallen asleep in the chair halfway through the first movie. Some party pooper I was. I guessed actually getting out and socializing had taken its toll. I looked at it this way—"resistance was futile." But I thought I still had some issues about relationships I didn't want to face.

I was in the kitchen making stuffed French toast for Wendy, Anna, Michelle and myself when Frances walked in.

"Hey! Join us for breakfast," I said.

"I'd love to, that looks fabulous. But I have an idea."

"Fire away."

"Well, with Wendy's guy in the Bahamas, why don't you and I go over to her house today and get all of his stuff out of it?"

I considered this as I readied the pan of stuffed French

toast for the oven. I had made it the night before and all I had to do now was slide it in, but I was just fussing with it, giving it a little more attention.

Think a rich caramel sauce of brown sugar and butter, then great bread dipped in eggs and half-and-half and spices, one slice placed on top of the caramel in the pan. Add a bunch of thinly sliced apples on top of each slice of bread, pile the fruit really high. Then you put another slice of egg-dipped bread over the top to make a kind of fruit pocket, then spices over it all and into the oven to bake and fill your kitchen with the most amazing smells…you get the picture.

Fattening and fabulous, I only made it on very special occasions. And since Wendy had survived her pity party, that counted as a special occasion to me.

At the end of the party last night, before I'd toddled off to bed, I'd told everyone what I'd done—I'd confessed to sending Mr. Married to the Bahamas.

Frances had shrieked with laughter, Ariel's eyes had widened in appreciation, Michelle had looked astonished and Wendy had thanked me. But Frances was right—with him out of the picture, it *was* the perfect time to get all traces of him out of Wendy's home. There was absolutely no chance he'd be around to cause any trouble.

"We'll fuel up on my French toast and then hit the road," I said.

* * *

Of course the French toast was a smashing success. I'd first enjoyed it at a bed-and-breakfast up in northern California, and shamelessly cajoled the recipe out of the owner.

Then Frances and Wendy and I headed out in my van. I'd offered to drive since I really didn't know how much of this guy's stuff was at Wendy's house. I figured with a van, there was no excuse for not getting all of it out today.

Once inside her home, Wendy went straight to her cat, Max, and made a huge fuss over him. Frances and I tackled the boxes.

"That book about breakups Ariel recommended is simply genius," Frances said as she reinforced the bottom of a large box with masking tape. One box was for any of his valuable stuff, which was obviously going back to him. The second was for all of the stuff he'd given to Wendy, any gifts. We'd also enclose any pictures, letters or other mementos that could cause her a moment's heartache. And the third box was for just plain trash.

The trash would be thrown out. The box of Wendy's was given to a friend (me), to be put up in an attic and not opened for at least a year. And the box of his valuables was what the actual breakup buddy (me and Frances today) was for; he or she would deliver it back to the boyfriend, so there was no contact at all between the two ex's.

It was essentially a packing party, and Wendy had offered to spring for pizza and beer. So she led us through the house and directed us to various things he had given her. I had to admit that, even though I believed that their relationship had truly sucked, he'd given her some exquisite jewelry. Though all those expensive gifts smacked of being kept. And it told me a lot about his guilt—or else he just had so much money that he spent it in order to keep Wendy on his hook.

I knew there were women out there who wouldn't mind such an arrangement, but I just couldn't see it. It had always struck me as a worthless sort of life.

I felt like we were helping Wendy toward a bright new future, eradicating any sign of this man. It would make things that much easier for her once she returned home.

"You know the other part of this," Frances said, placing a packet of letters into Wendy's box. "The part about changing your home around, painting a wall, rearranging the furniture. Just doing anything so that the place doesn't remind you of him. That was also brilliant. I wish I'd had this book right after my divorce."

"I talked with Wendy about that," I said. "She has a friend who's an interior designer who's volunteered to come in and move everything around. This guy is one of those people who can take all the old pieces, add one or two more, and essentially give you a new decorating scheme."

"I've never been much good at that. Maybe I could hire him to come take a look at my place," Frances mused.

"I just went with what I loved."

"Your place is so cozy."

I got that a lot and I didn't mind it. I've always been the den mother type to all my friends. I didn't mind it with friends, but I didn't want that with a man.

We broke for pizza at around two in the afternoon, and the three of us agreed we were almost eighty percent done. After a quick lunch, we really hauled and got the rest of it finished in record time. By the time we stepped back and surveyed the results, we had about four boxes of trash, two that belonged to him, and a large one that belonged to Wendy.

Eight years in seven boxes; almost a box per year.

"You're sure you two don't mind dropping his stuff off?" Wendy asked as we drove back to my house.

"Not at all. What's a breakup buddy for?" I said.

"We were thinking about doing it tonight, while he's still out of town," said Frances.

"The sooner the better," Wendy replied.

I was so proud of her. Her Achilles' heel had been hearing his voice on the phone and listening to all his pleading and false promises. Now that I was in charge of her cell phone, that problem had been solved. Even better, after our little cleanup, she had nothing to remind her of him.

She was so ambitious in this breakup, wiping him out of her life on such a grand scale, it wouldn't have surprised me if she'd put her house on the market, bought something else and started over.

We dropped Wendy off at my house and took off again, heading toward the Westside and Pacific Palisades. By the time we reached Married Man's neighborhood, I understood how he'd been able to buy Wendy all that jewelry.

The house we pulled up in front of was an enormous faux Tudor, the dark wood stunning against the white plaster. The landscaping was top of the line, and the car parked in the driveway was a black, late model Mercedes sedan.

"How exactly do we do this?" I said as I cut the van's engine and the two of us sat looking at the house. Now that we were actually here, I was nervous. It had to be done, but I didn't want to cause anyone in Married Man's family any emotional pain. And that was a little naïve of me because, of course, that was exactly what Frances and I were about to do.

Yet we had to help Wendy make a totally clean break. And it would have been petty of her to throw his stuff away.

"Too bad we don't have his work address," Frances muttered, staring at the faux Tudor.

"We should have thought of that," I said. "Should we call Wendy?"

"No, I think we should get it over with."

But neither of us made the first move to get out of my van.

The big question was, did Married Man's wife know about his affair? Or was she in total denial, trying to look the other way for the sake of keeping the peace? Either way, Frances and I were about to barge into her world and do some serious damage.

"Double-check that address. I want to make sure we only do this once." Frances hesitated. "Eva, have you ever done anything like this before?"

"Nope."

"So there aren't any rules or protocol to follow."

"None that I know of," I said. "All I know is that Wendy can't do it."

"Amen to that." Frances replied.

I checked the address Wendy had given us against the one in front of us,then checked it again. I knew I was stalling. I really hate stuff like this. Do married men ever stop and think about all the lives they're about to destroy when they give in to that temptation—their wives, their children, their extended families? Well, of course they don't.

And it wasn't exactly a one-night stand; it had been eight years of temptation, plenty of time for this guy to reconsider his actions. The whole affair had only come to an end once Wendy had the emotional courage to end it.

I sighed. I felt awful. "We're at the right address."

"Do you want me to do this alone?" Frances said.

"Hell, no. I want to get a look at this woman." That sounded shallow as hell, but I had to admit I was curious.

"Do you think she knows?"

I thought about this for a moment. "Let me put it this way, I don't think Wendy was this jerk's first affair, and I'm sure she won't be his last. The only way his wife can ride this out is either if she accepts it completely and sees it as the price she has to pay for her lifestyle with him, or if she lives in denial."

Frances was silent for a moment, then said, "I'm voting for her accepting it completely. Denial's pretty hard to maintain in the face of a box of evidence."

"No kidding."

Silence for a few more minutes, the Frances said, "Let's get this over with," and opened her door.

We got out of the car, and I just prayed we wouldn't hear the sound of young children playing inside the house, or find any toys strewn around the front door. If they had any little kids, it would only make things worse. He had his two daughters, Wendy had mentioned them, but perhaps they were adolescents and old enough to be out of the house a great deal of the time. They didn't need to see this.

We walked up to the front door, each of us carrying a box. Frances rang the doorbell and we waited. After a few seconds, we heard the sound of someone coming toward the door. My stomach knotted. Frances didn't look so good herself.

A Hispanic woman in a crisp pink maid's uniform answered the door. In absolutely flawless Spanish, Frances politely asked her if the *señora* was home.

"I keep meaning to learn Spanish," I muttered beneath my breath as the woman turned around and headed back inside the house. My heart was pounding so fast I had to take a deep breath to steady myself. For one insane moment I wanted to leave all the stuff on her front step and make a run for it.

How incredibly mature.

"It's not all that hard."

What? Oh yeah, learning Spanish.

I wasn't quite sure what was going to happen, but it couldn't be good. At this point, I just wanted this whole thing over with.

In a way, our timing was perfect. Married Man was frantically searching for Wendy in the Bahamas. When he came home and found that all his stuff had been dumped back at his house, he would have to take this as a jumbo hint and realize the whole thing was over. Maybe he'd even stop calling and leave Wendy alone.

Maybe Frances and I could look at what we were doing in a positive light. Perhaps it would give Married Man the wakeup call he needed.

Yeah right.

The woman who came to the door was stick thin with enormous breasts that obviously weren't the originals. Her hair was too blond, her thin face too tan, and she had a worried, anxious look in her blue eyes that really got to me. She looked far too young to have any children, let alone two daughters. Maybe they were from Married Man's first marriage.

For one insane moment I thought she was one of his daughters, but then I really looked at her eyes and they told me all I needed to know. This woman had a defeated, resigned kind of energy. It was clear she knew about her husband, probably tried to accept it and deal with it, but the whole pack of lies caused her a lot of grief. You could see it in her face, the tension she carried, the lines around her eyes.

"Hi," said Frances softly, so gently, setting down her

box on the small bench by the front door. I did the same. "We're friends of a—a friend of your husband's and—we're returning all of the stuff your husband left at her house." She hesitated, seemingly at a loss for words, then said quickly, "I'm sorry that we had to give you this news."

Something in those china blue eyes shifted, and she said, her voice merely a whisper, "Thank you." And I realized that if I had met this woman at another place, at another time, I would've liked her.

Sometimes life just sucks.

"Is it over for good?" the woman asked Frances.

"Yes," she said.

"Was it one of you?"

"No," I answered.

She nodded her head and looked so tired. And I knew that the house, the car, the maid, all of it came at a terrible price to her spirit.

I just couldn't stand this. "If I were you, I'd sell all his stuff on eBay." Remember how I said that sometimes I open my mouth and stuff my foot all the way in?

But the woman smiled, the tiniest of smiles, and it was genuine. It reached those tired blue eyes.

"I just might do that."

We all looked at each other for a moment longer, then she said, "Well, I guess that's it."

"Yeah. I'm really sorry," said Frances, and the two of us started back to the van.

We were almost halfway home, each of us in our own thoughts, when Frances said, "Will she be okay? What do you think's going to happen when he gets home? I feel so bad for her."

"I know. I did, too. But I think she knew."

"Yeah, I got the same feeling."

I considered all that we'd just seen, then said, "I think she's going to sell some of it, but if she does, she'll leave just enough so he knows she knows. I'd hate a setup like that for myself, but if she's smart, she'll bury him in guilt for a month or two."

Frances considered this, then said, "Good."

Our next meeting of the I Hate to Date Club got off to a rip-roaring start.

"You're not going to believe this!" Ariel said. She'd asked for the floor first, and we were all looking forward to the tales of her adventures in her new power suit. Power Girl, Master of her Domain (not in the Seinfeld sense).

"C'mon, spill it," Frances said from one of the couches.

"Okay. Get this! Michelle helped me buy my suit on Tuesday evening. Actually, we bought two suits, but I decided to wear the one I was planning to wear on Saturday to the office so that it wouldn't look too brand new, you know what I mean?"

We all followed her logic easily.

"So my boss must have told me I looked terrific about ten times, and I decided to wear the other suit on Thursday. And on Friday, when I wore the original suit with a different blouse, he asked me to come into his office and gave me a promotion!"

"*What?*" I said. "Why didn't you tell us Friday night?"

She smiled, clearly enjoying the moment. "I wanted to save it for our meeting. Michelle, you were so right, we have so much control over how other people see us. I know that this new look got me a better job! I think he saw me as more businesslike and authoritative."

"Great!" Wendy said. "But what happened with the writing group?"

"This is the *best* part," Ariel said. She was standing in front of all of us, a bundle of energy, and I knew she had to be absolutely stunning when she pitched her screenplays. Her enthusiasm was that contagious.

"Okay. I leave here Saturday morning, after our party. Michelle's done a masterful job with my hair and makeup, and given me quite the little pep talk. So I drive to West Hollywood, time it perfectly, and breeze into our coffee shop on La Cienega barely ten minutes late."

"And Nate?" Frances asked.

"Michelle, you were so right, he couldn't take his eyes off me! And all of them bought my bogus story about an early-morning meeting with an author, like a breakfast thing. So we sat and talked about how our writing went that week, but Nate just kept staring."

"He's going to find a way to change the relationship," I predicted. "No more of this best-friend stuff."

"Though it would be nice to be best friends with a man you also loved," Michelle said.

"Yeah, I can see that," Wendy said.

"So, Operation Power Suit was a huge success! Now I just wait and see what happens but stay busy in the meantime. And I want to buy a few more suits for work. After all, I have to live up to my new job!"

"I'll shop with you anytime," Michelle said. "But we should do it early this next week in case something comes up for me with work."

I thought of John Dempsey and what he'd said about getting her a job on his next movie. I had a feeling Michelle would be working before long.

Ariel made a great show of crossing out her date on the calendar, after writing in "success" in huge yellow letters and pasting on a glittery gold star.

"I also went to the gallery opening and managed to give my number to two really nice men who both asked for it. Neither have called, but don't you think they'll probably call early this coming week for next weekend?"

"Yep," I said.

"And then, of course, Wednesday. Wendy, I'm so proud of you!"

"Not yet," Wendy said. "Ariel, let's keep the focus on you. Where do you want to go from here? What goals do you want to set for next week?"

"Okay. I've got two guys that might call. I'm going to a talk Tuesday night at the Writer's Guild of America. Those screenwriting things have nothing but men attending, so I'll look great and see who I can get to take my number. At least we'd have writing in common. Also, I want to see what's going to happen with Nate. He may even come to this talk with me."

"Okay," Frances said. "So, people, does the night at the Writer's Guild of America count as Ariel's date?"

"Yeah," said Michelle. "She's putting herself out there, maintaining her image at work, Nate may call, those other two may call—I'd say get yourself a good calendar, one of those month-at-a-glance things that fits in your bag."

"And I *feel* great," Ariel said. "Like I'm more noticeable. The bolder colors did the trick, Michelle!"

"I only aim to please."

"I'm done!" Ariel said, flinging herself into an overstuffed chair.

"Okay. Eva?" said Frances.

"I went to the gallery and didn't get any men to take my number, but I avoided getting involved with a man when I found out he already had a girlfriend. I cut that one off at the knees. I don't have time for that kind of stuff."

"Good girl," said Ariel.

I thought about mentioning meeting John Dempsey and decided not to. I'd keep quiet about what I thought might be going on with him and Michelle.

"Michelle highlighted and cut my hair and showed me how to do some new makeup stuff. We went out and bought several outfits, so I feel like I'm good to go if I get invited anywhere. I really feel great about how I look now."

"Any possibilities with the catering?" Wendy asked.

"The next job is a birthday party. A dinner for the whole family for Grandpa's eightieth birthday."

"Well, you *are* at that age..." Michelle said, letting her voice trail off.

Everyone laughed and I threw a pillow at her. "Okay, I'm open to any invitations anyone would care to throw my way. In the meantime, any suggestions as to where I could meet someone?"

"Starbucks is supposed to be the hot new place to meet men," Wendy said. "I read it in the *L.A. Times.*"

"No!" said Michelle. "Don't give her any excuse to bury her head in a book and sip a cappuccino!"

"Good point," Frances said. "Why don't we brainstorm at the end of the meeting to see what kind of invites we can come up with? But in the meantime, let's congratulate Eva on getting out of the house!"

Cheers and clapping ensued, and I sat down feeling that I'd done my part for the world of dating.

Wendy was next. She thanked all of us profusely for helping her on Wednesday night, then said she was taking it day by day. She also reported that all of Married Man's things had been returned, thanks to Frances and me. Then she told the group—actually, Ariel—that her serious mementos from the affair were boxed up and locked upstairs in my attic in case she had a weak moment and wanted to think about Married Man and make him out to be much more than he was.

I'd insisted that she move all the good jewelry to her safe-deposit box at her bank because I didn't feel safe with it packed in a box in my attic. I thought of all that money in jewels as her payment for all the shit she'd put up with. Crass, I know, but practical. At least she came out of it with something.

My guess was that every time she tried to leave or he felt guilty, she got a new piece of jewelry. It was quite the collection.

Wendy also told the group about the interior designer who was going to take a look at her home and rearrange things so that when she moved back in she wouldn't think of Rick every time she turned around.

She was just destroying memories right and left, and we were behind her every step of the way.

"I'm taking a ten-day break from work," Wendy said. "I want to really take care of myself through this process, eat well, catch up on sleep, see some movies, go shopping, get my head on straight. I've been working too hard for the last few years, and now I feel it was because I sensed the whole thing with Rick was going nowhere. I kept myself busy so I wouldn't have to think."

That was a stellar bit of insight. I was impressed.

"So your goals for the next two weeks?" Frances said. Ariel sat by the coffee table, thick blue marker pen poised over the calendar.

"More of the same, just daily emotional survival. Anna gave me a journal—you all know that—and I've been writing every day. One of the things I wrote about was—I made this list of all the things I put on hold while I was involved with Rick. All sorts of things I want to do now that I don't have to think about him."

"Excellent!" I said, and really meant it. Wendy was plunging ahead at the speed of light.

"I think I'm going to make a list of all the things I gave up when I was with Bryan," said Michelle.

"I like the thought of a list like that," said Frances. "I'm going to work on one, too."

"The trick," I interjected, "is to be in a relationship but to not give up those parts of yourself. Why does being in a relationship have to mean that a woman diminishes herself?"

"I'm glad I inspired you all," said Wendy. "That's it for me."

"That's a *lot*," said Ariel. "You may not see it, but you've come a long way from the first day we all met at Starbucks."

"I couldn't have done it without you guys."

"Now Michelle!" I said.

Everyone agreed, and Michelle, looking just a little uneasy, said, "You all asked me to think of something that I wanted at the next meeting. Frances, I'd like you to refer me to a really great divorce lawyer. Bryan's dragging his feet and doing nothing, and I don't really want to delay the inevitable any longer than necessary. It's so stupid, it's like when a guy acts out badly and is completely passive-aggressive so that you'll finally break up with him. I just want to get the whole damn thing over with. Would that be all right?"

"More than all right. But how about something fun?"

"I guess, for now, just being included in any of the

group invites. I used to work so hard, then any extra time I had I tried to spend with my soon-to-be ex. Eva's really the only close friend I had before this group formed. So just think of me when you plan your outings, that would make me happy."

She sat back, and I said, "Okay, Frances, you're next."

I could tell something was wrong the minute she started to speak.

"Don't get me wrong, guys. I love this group, and I adore all of you. I think that first meeting jump-started me in a way that I haven't been pushed in years, and it felt good. It felt right. But I'm not sure that I want to date right now, and if I'm not in a space to date, I guess I really shouldn't be here."

"What?" I said, hating the thought of losing Frances.

"What is it you feel you want to do?" Wendy said.

"I want to paint," Frances said quietly. "I painted more in this last week than the entire month! I finished the canvas I was working on and started another. And going to that gallery opening, it made me want an opening of my own!"

"That's an admirable goal to work toward," Ariel said. "I don't see why you have to be kicked out of the group because you want to direct your energies into your art instead of a man."

"It's like I want to work on *myself*," Frances continued. "You know how Wendy wants to stay away from Rick for sixty days and then reassess where she is? I'd love to simply *paint* for sixty days and then reevaluate where I am with my life. I think I need to get back all that I lost in my marriage."

"You didn't paint when you were married?" Michelle asked.

"No. I worked hellishly long hours, my life was totally out of balance, and all my supplies stayed shut in this one cupboard in our house. I was miserable, and I didn't know why. Then one day, about eight months after my divorce became final, I got out all my oils and started painting again."

"I think it's a great idea, to paint for sixty days," Wendy said. "I think you should go with your feelings. If you want to paint, that's what you should do. Forget dating. And we all still want you here in the group."

"So I can stay?" Frances said, looking relieved.

"Hey, Wendy isn't dating right now," I said. "Neither is Michelle. But they're still both members, right?"

"Right!" Ariel said. "Eva and I will do enough dating for the entire group!"

Speak for yourself. You have two men from the gallery, Nate from the coffee shop and an entire room of lusty male screenwriters to pick from. Me, I can hardly get the ball rolling in a gallery full of men.

"Of course!" I said. No way did I want Frances leaving the group.

"So, what are your painting goals?" Ariel said, picking up her red pen.

"I'm going to try and paint twenty hours a week, six on Tuesday and Thursday, and a full eight on Saturday. And I'm going to call a few friends and check out their galleries, see what it takes to mount a show. I figure I can make up a notebook and break the whole thing down into steps so it isn't quite so intimidating."

"Or one of us could do it for you," Ariel said. "Sometimes it's easier to have someone else sell you, or ask all the questions."

"That would be great!" Frances replied.

We were all happy with our goals that day, so we ended the meeting on a high note and I brought out the turkey chili I'd made the day before. Here's a huge, huge catering secret that any good cook knows. All soups and stews, chilies and spaghetti sauces tasted so much better if they were made the day before the event. It gave the flavors time to blend.

So we enjoyed the chili and the cheese and jalapeño corn bread along with a spinach salad I'd thrown together. Taking after my mother, I made sure that everyone had a green vegetable. I'd been in a bit of a hurry, so dessert was one-pan brownies with a great vanilla ice cream and homemade chocolate sauce.

"You spoil us, Eva," Frances said as she spooned up the last of her ice cream. "I look forward to these meals with you guys all week."

"I was thinking of creating some fast meals for you when you're in the middle of your painting so you don't have to leave it too long."

"I'd love that."

Before we knew it, Ariel and Frances had left, and Michelle, Wendy and I were still in the living room, talking.

Then Michelle's cell phone rang and she answered it. "Hey, John," she said, then stood up and walked out of the living room.

"John?" Wendy said. "A new guy?"

"An old friend," I said truthfully. "I think he was going to call her about a job."

Sure enough, when Michelle came back into the living room, it was to tell us that she'd gotten the job and would be leaving for Hawaii at the end of the week.

"See?" I said, teasing Wendy. "And here you thought the house would be too crowded if you came and stayed for a while. If you hadn't, Anna and I would be rattling around like two peas in an enormous pod."

"I just love her, Eva," Wendy said. "She's been like a

mother to me. She's one of the most fabulous women I've ever met."

"I agree with that," Michelle said. She frowned. "I'm going to have to talk to Frances tomorrow and get that lawyer's name, I'd like to start the ball rolling before I leave."

It struck me, as I sat there and watched my friends talk, that everyone seemed to have so much to do but me. I had my job, but at that moment I felt like I wasn't really moving forward in my life.

I'd reached the point with my catering business where I could do the majority of the work blindfolded. This wasn't to say that I was bored; I was one of those people always trying new recipes, watching the Food Channel for ideas and inspiration, making sure the work stayed interesting.

For a moment, I even considered signing up for a ten-day cooking class in another country, maybe Italy. I felt as if I had to get my heart back in the right place. Maybe I needed jump-starting, as Frances had called it. I had to find my North Star.

So much had happened in just two weeks—to everyone but me.

Wendy had made such strides since the breakup. Michelle would be working again, and was starting divorce proceedings. Frances was all fired up about her painting. Ariel was flying along with her own personal schedule, she'd just gotten a promotion and I had the distinct feeling she'd have a date for this weekend by Wednesday at the latest.

And I was beginning to realize how unbalanced and limited my life had become.

Patience, I counseled myself as I watched Michelle and Wendy talking on the couch. Then Anna came into the living room, a cup of tea in her hands and Ming at her heels. She asked us how the meeting had gone. I sat back and listened as they told her all the exciting news.

I couldn't complain. I had my health, good friends, a wonderful home, terrific companion animals and a creative career I adored. But somewhere in the mix was the smallest voice of doubt, a voice that seriously posed the question I didn't even want to acknowledge, let alone answer.

What if there simply wasn't anyone out there for me?

CHAPTER 12

My private pity party lasted all of one evening. When I woke up the following morning, I realized that I was being ridiculous. Only two weeks had gone by since we'd started the I Hate to Date Club, and in that time I'd managed to highlight my hair and get out of the house to a gallery opening. So what if I hadn't had any luck with the single men there? It was all a numbers game, as Ariel kept telling me. I decided to stop being so hard on myself and take it easy.

It was always that way. Almost every woman I knew had a story about a friend or a sister, someone who finally said, "That's it! I'm done with men! I'm letting the whole thing go!" And that's when the right man walked straight into her life.

How many women do we all know who finally let the dream of children go after trying to conceive for years? And a lot of times, when they surrendered, that was the exact moment they got pregnant.

So I decided to surrender. It was kind of like losing

weight. You didn't get to your highest weight in a few weeks, and you didn't lose it in a healthy way in a short amount of time. It took some major rethinking and a touch of strategy to make your life make sense again.

In a nutshell, I was expecting results too fast. That was the problem in America; none of us wanted to wait for anything. Our collective ability to delay gratification was laughable. It was the reason I had the job I had, as most people didn't want to put the time, effort and thought into creating really wonderful food.

So I made peace with where I was, and realized that I didn't get to my single, dateless, manless existence overnight, and the problem couldn't be fixed in the same amount of time.

One of the things we all agreed upon at the end of the first meeting that I forgot to mention was that we decided to keep the concept of our club a total secret. There were many reasons for this, the major one being that many of our female friends were of the opinion that a woman didn't need a man to make her life complete. And they would see this club as a total negation of that great truth.

It was true that no one should ever be totally defined by another person. But the rest of that truth, as I saw it, was that we were communal creatures. There's not a person I knew who really loved to eat alone, day after day. The problems that life inevitably threw at you were easier faced with someone you could trust and depend on at your side.

So we all made the conscious decision that we'd support each other, but we didn't want any other women looking inside our group and directing any negative thoughts or opinions toward us.

I was all for it. In the back of my mind I felt a little self-conscious that I was in my late thirties and still didn't have this whole dating-man-partnership thing under control.

So, life went on. Michelle and Ariel went shopping and Ariel's wardrobe became a thing of great beauty. Michelle left for Hawaii at the end of the week, I drove her to LAX and she caught her flight out. Frances holed up in her light-filled studio in Silverlake and painted her heart out. Wendy continued to write in her journal and rest. She and Anna formed a bond so swiftly; it was as if Anna had found the daughter she'd always wished she had.

I wasn't jealous. Anna and I had a deep friendship, but it was almost as if Anna and Wendy had known each other before and had just started up the relationship again. I always found them deep in conversation when I entered a room, or else sitting over tea in the break-fast nook.

It was funny the way things had worked out—I was sure that, given a chance, many people would have told me I was a fool to have so many people stay at my house.

Michelle had had the run of my house since the years I'd slept on a mattress and used a laundry basket for a dresser. Anna had always been so good to me, I simply couldn't bear the thought of her being isolated way out in Riverside and waiting for death. And Wendy—something about her had touched me, from the first evening after our reading group when she'd asked if we could talk. She'd reached out, and I'd seen the need and decided to answer it.

Sometimes life really was that simple.

In my quest to get out of the house more, I'd joined Anna and Wendy for a movie, a foreign film that Married Man would have never wanted to see. It was French, and a comedy, and we all loved it. Afterward, having coffee and tea at the café at Vromann's, we talked.

"It's always more complicated than people think," Anna said. "I like the way the writer didn't settle for an easy answer, and that the characters were lovable in spite of their flaws."

"Very human flaws," I added.

"Do we expect too much?" Wendy asked.

"I think in some ways, yes," said Anna. "I think it was

simpler when I was married because no one expected their husbands to fill up all the empty spaces. He was as overwhelmed making a living as I was raising our two children. There were years where I felt we both barely had our heads above water, we'd kind of meet in the middle, acknowledge each other, and keep on working. But I never thought that it was his job to make me happy. I knew I had to do that for myself."

"Is that what's wrong with romance?" I said. "I mean, the way it's depicted in the movies and in books."

"Not in real romance," Anna said. "In the best stories, the characters have to fight the odds to find happiness, and no one does that sort of work for them. They are whole in themselves before they get the relationship."

"Do you think we've become lazy as a culture?" said Wendy.

"I don't know," Anna replied. "I think we want things faster, every day things seem to speed up. No one seems to have time for the little things anymore, the things that used to make life worth living. I can remember evenings when the kids were finally in bed, and my husband would take out a deck of cards and we would play and laugh, have a glass of wine and talk. It made me feel close to him, that he wanted to spend time with me. And the rest of our relationship just flowed from little moments like that."

"I wish I could find a man like that," Wendy said.

"They're out there. But sometimes, in this day and age, I think the woman has to be the one to pull the deck of cards out of her purse and slow everything down."

"Why do we think we don't have time?" I said, really curious now.

"There's a very simple answer to that question," Anna said. "What you value, you make time for. When my husband made time for me, after all the other things we had to do to keep our lives functioning, I felt valued. And when you feel valued, you feel loved."

I glanced over at Wendy and saw that her eyes had filled. She looked down at her coffee and shaded her face with one hand.

"You feel what you need to feel," Anna said fiercely, her arm coming up around Wendy's delicate shoulders.

What a great mother hen Anna was.

"I just—I want to stay honest, because it's the only way this whole thing is bearable," Wendy whispered. "What you said about your husband just now made me realize that Rick never valued me."

I was about to say *I'm sure there were moments*, but I bit my tongue and forced myself to silence.

"No man values a woman when he lies to her."

There. Just like that, Anna got to the heart of the

problem. And she probably helped Wendy a lot more than all the reassurance ever would.

We sat in silence in the sunlight for a long moment, letting Wendy gather her emotions back together. I knew I was a lucky woman to live here and have the leisure time to sit at a café table with friends and discuss our lives and the world we lived in.

"I'm okay," Wendy finally said. "I'd like to keep talking for a while, it's so nice just sitting here and relaxing."

"Not something you do that often?" Anna said.

"No. When I'm in Europe, I'm usually working."

"Raymond and I took a trip to Rome after our youngest child left for college. We'd saved our change for years in a big jar in the kitchen, and in the evenings we would sit together and roll all the coins into those holders. Once a month he'd take the money to the bank and put it in our savings account."

"How long did you do that?" I said. Anna was one of those women who always surprised you with her stories. You thought you knew her, yet every time she would show you new depths.

"We started right after we got married. His mother advised us to do it. She said we could save a significant amount, and that we should put it in the bank and eventually spend it on a dream that the two of us could share."

"That's lovely," Wendy said.

"We decided to take a trip to Italy. He had relatives in Rome we could stay with. We bought travel books and kept a little notebook filled with all the things we were going to see once we got there."

"Was it everything you expected it to be?" I asked.

"And so much more. It was such a wonderful trip, and the timing was right. Our last child had left, and we needed to become a couple again."

"It sounded like you two remained pretty close even through all the difficult years." I admired Anna for the strong bond she and her husband had created.

"We did. But that trip—it was like the icing on a cake. We saw so much beautiful art, the paintings and the sculptures. And the food! We ate out almost every evening, or at least went for coffee. And we took the train up to Florence and Venice."

I glanced at Wendy and thought of last Christmas Eve, when Rick had promised to meet her in London

"I know I was lucky," said Anna quietly. "I still am."

Lucky? With a daughter like hers who simply wanted to warehouse her own mother, lock her away where no one could get to her? With a son I'd never really heard much about? How did two people like Anna and her husband, Raymond, end up with offspring like those two?

I had never bought into the whole thing espoused in this country that it was all the parents' fault. When I was growing up back in the Midwest, I'd seen great parents with crappy kids and crappy parents with terrific kids. A lot could be said for nurturing, but when push came to shove, it was the luck of the draw.

I had never been one of those women who had this overwhelming biological clock. To be perfectly honest, I was only looking as far ahead in my future as a great, solid relationship with a man. Children didn't even enter the picture for me.

Michelle would have wanted children if things had gone differently for her. The last few years of her marriage, she and Bryan were—or at least she—was really trying. I knew one of the most painful tragedies of her life would be if she never had a child of her own.

Me, I've just never felt that way. I'm fortunate to have parents who never pushed the matter, and I've had a lot of relatives like my great-aunt who never had kids and lived a very full life, so the example was always there for me.

"What did you want to do, Anna?" Wendy asked suddenly.

"What do you mean?"

"Something besides your family. Besides being a wife and mother. Did you ever have any big dreams?"

And Anna smiled, a smile I'd never seen before, as if she was conjuring up wonderful memories right here at the little café table.

"I wanted to be a designer."

"Like a fashion designer?" I said.

"Yes."

She talked a little longer, and Wendy and I listened. We listened to stories of her making all her children's clothing, of Raymond coming home from work and stopping off at a newsstand to buy her a copy of *Vogue*. He'd never laughed at her dreams, never discouraged her, but both of them had been so busy with their everyday lives.

She described dresses she'd made for friends as if she'd just sewn the final hem the day before; the styles, the fabrics, the colors. Wendy leaned in to listen, and as she was a part of the world of fashion, I saw immediately how these two had connected even more.

At about three in the afternoon I reminded the two of them that I had to head home and get organized for the big birthday bash for Grandpa tonight. A home in San Marino with a gorgeous formal dining room, and a happy family celebrating their elderly patriarch's milestone year. They'd opted for classic food—standing rib roast and Yorkshire pudding, a green veg and a vanilla cream cake that would be loaded with sparklers. The final effect in the dark dining room would be truly spectacular.

I always liked doing birthdays—they're generally happy celebrations.

"Then we should go," Anna said, quickly finishing the last of her green tea. "Do you need help with tonight?"

"Not really, but I'd love the company."

"Could I come?" Wendy asked. "I won't get in the way."

"Sure." It would be good to keep her busy. Wendy had been so strong during the aftermath of her breakup, but she hadn't reached that sixty-day marker yet. All of us were keeping a close eye on her until then.

The birthday party was a huge success, the family a delight. I had a feeling they'd be calling me for other jobs. One of my favorite types of jobs, just nice people, never a moment of trouble. They went in a special section of my work files, under "Clients I definitely want to work with again."

Anna turned out to be a great help. Wendy was completely fascinated by the whole process. She helped me plate up and serve the family as I carved, and I caught Gramps sneaking her an admiring glance. It wasn't sleazy at all, just a male admiring a beautiful woman. They were visual creatures, after all. Some things never change.

Michelle called and let me know she was all settled in and getting ready to go down to the beach for a surfing lesson before the rush of work began. Now, *that's* what I considered a great job. Frances checked in every so often, and decided to hire me to prepare some food for her and deliver it so she could continue painting nonstop.

Wendy called her agency and said she'd be ready for work at the end of the ten days she'd taken off from her life, and Ariel had a total of two dates for the weekend—Nate and one of the guys from the gallery, Ted.

And *moi?* Since Michelle was no longer here and keeping an eye out for my social life—or lack of one— I decided to go to my local Borders on Lake Street and pick up a few books. Maybe I'd really be naughty and have a coffee. Perhaps there was some way I could convince everyone at the next meeting that this counted as a social event.

Hey, for me, it did.

January faded into February, and there was one event that gave me a great deal of joy. We had our reading group, and I actually read and enjoyed the book we'd selected. But the big event was Paige having a meltdown because she really liked *Winter Solstice.*

It was the strangest thing. I don't think she knew

what to do, or how to respond to a book that hadn't been preapproved by Oprah.

"I actually really *liked* this book!" she said, an anxious look on her usually smooth face. Even her usually flawless blonde hair seemed nervous.

"Do you think it was because the heroine actually had a life and made some really powerful decisions and she didn't end up dead?" I said, reaching for a piece of Scottish shortbread I'd made earlier that day. What with the gorgeous, wild Scottish setting for most of the novel, I was thankful that Paige hadn't attempted to make haggis. Or have us wear plaid.

Phil, the one guy in our group, wouldn't have even considered a kilt.

"It's strange how so many books have women characters that are punished in the end," Frances remarked. "This novel had the most uplifting ending, I actually had tears in my eyes when I finished it."

"Sometimes I don't think our culture's come all that far when it comes to women," Ariel added. "It's like we aren't even allowed to have pleasure. I mean, really, who does it hurt?"

"And I *loved* the fact that the heroine was older!" Wendy said. "It's like saying that a woman can actually have a life into her fifties, sixties and seventies, even beyond. I mean, try finding that in today's movies."

"They want teenage boys' butts in the seats at the multiplex," Ariel said. "The Industry's all about the money, honey, except for the artists who actually want to create something great." She reached for another piece of shortbread. "Eva, this is so good."

"Would the group be open to more books like this one?" Wendy said, directing her question toward Paige.

We all turned toward her, totally attentive. The other members of the group had all loved *Winter Solstice*, but I had the feeling that the final decision would be up to our leader. I could only hope for the best—I might actually want to read some of our selections.

It was the strangest thing. We'd clearly taken Paige way out of her comfort zone. And I realized that, for her, reading a novel was all about *work*. She had a very strong work ethic, and at that moment I just got it that reading a book for pleasure, just for the sheer fun of it, had been a totally new experience for her.

If we'd suggested one of Janet Evanovich's Stephanie Plum series, she might have imploded.

"Well, I suppose—" she began, then hesitated.

I glanced at Ariel. Her dark eyes twinkled, then she said, "You know, Paige, this book really inspired me. I mean, look at all the negative messages women get about aging. And look at the way the heroine dealt with all the challenges thrown her way. I really believe it was a book about coping with grief, and going on, and really living. Didn't you learn a lot from reading it?"

I picked up the baton before Paige could answer. "Yeah, it was like I felt like I really *worked* for some of the answers. Like in reading about the characters I thought about how *I* would rise to those challenges. Pilcher asked some tough questions, put her characters in some really hard places. But I learned from it, and I felt like I grew." I hoped I hadn't piled it on too thick, like with a trowel.

It worked. I could almost see her releasing the guilt. The expression in her eyes shifted, and she glanced around. "But it was also such a good *story!*"

"Oh, I know," said Frances, and as she continued to expound, Ariel looked at me and mouthed, *Good work.* Then we both turned our attention back to the discussion. And I wondered about Paige, who couldn't seem to let herself read for sheer, unadulterated enjoyment.

Well, we'd fix that. If not this time, then later in the year.

In the end, we reached a great compromise. Paige picked the March selection, the Sylvia Plath biography she'd been dying to read. Another one of the women had wanted to read a historical novel in April. But Wendy could select our May book.

"Thanks, Paige," said Wendy as we were all leaving,

Ziploc bags of shortbread in everyone's hands. "Like I said last month, I just needed a little break from the sort of stories we'd been reading. I'm sure the Plath bio will be just wonderful."

In my mind, I was already in line at my Blockbuster on Fair Oaks, renting *Sylvia*, the movie starring Gwyneth Paltrow, along with a couple of romantic comedies.

But I could compromise, as well. I promised myself that on my next trip to Borders, I would pick up the Plath bio and give it a real try.

Of course, as singles, all of us moved into one of the most dreaded times of the year for the unpaired—Valentine's Day.

My social calendar was packed, if work counted. Anna and Wendy had volunteered to help, so I'd accepted three jobs. A lovers' breakfast, a husband's romantic brunch out by the pool for his wife of seven years, and—this one really had to go perfectly—a fabulously intimate and romantic dinner at a man's home. He was pulling out all the stops because he was going to ask his girlfriend of two years to marry him.

He'd even hired a small string quartet, so you knew the man was serious.

We had a quick meeting of our club before V-Day.

"Ugh, I just hate it," Frances said. "Valentine's Day

and New Year's Eve—the two toughest times to be single."

"How about Thanksgiving and going home to the family?" said Ariel. "Facing all those questions like, 'How come you're still single? Are you gay or something?'"

"Did your folks actually *say* that to you?" I said.

"No. But my cousin did, right at the table as I was dishing her out some green-bean casserole."

We all laughed, it was so typical of the stuff families pulled.

"Hey, Christmas is no picnic," I threw in. "It seems like everyone's paired off and happy, even all those reindeer."

"Fourth of July," Frances said wistfully. "Kissing in the dark while watching the fireworks."

Now we were getting silly.

"Halloween!" Ariel said. "Having to plan a costume for just one sucks."

"Mother's Day!" I called out, and everyone laughed. "Oh, wait, that's the tough one if you want to have children and still haven't done the deed."

"I think we've covered just about every major holiday except President's Day," said Frances. "We should get back on track."

"A holiday that can be surprisingly sexy if you put

your mind to it," I said, shamelessly trying to stall. This last two weeks had gotten away from me, with a lot of work and absolutely no effort made toward dating. I'd be facing the equivalent of a firing squad soon, and these women would offer me no mercy. The three of them were as bad as Michelle.

Ariel reported in first. She was dating three men at the same time, with Nate currently in the lead. She'd given out her phone number to two more men this week at a cocktail party she'd been invited to, had signed up for a writing class at UCLA Extension that was predominantly male, and had decided to try something called speed dating.

Just hearing about all that activity made me want to lie down on the couch, put my feet up and take a nap.

"I think you should come with me for some speed dating, Eva."

With my horrible two weeks of little to no effort coming up, I saw no way out. "That sounds great," I made myself say, forcing a smile. Wendy was the only one who looked at me a little oddly—you can't get much past her emotionally.

Frances was making great strides in her painting. She'd hired me to feed her and Ariel to do research and represent her. Her new goal was to have a show of her own by the spring.

"That's pretty ambitious," I said, "but absolutely attainable." I was beginning to see how I'd have to get serious about setting some goals. Or was I just fooling myself that I even wanted a relationship?

"Wendy?" Frances said, and Ariel rummaged in her bag for the blue marker.

"I want to give something back," she said softly.

That caught everyone's attention.

"I'm leaving for Milan at the end of the month, for three weeks," she said. "And while all of you have been there for me since the breakup, Anna has been my absolute rock."

I knew the feeling.

"I'm going to ask her to come with me and spend those three weeks in Italy, all expenses paid."

It was such an incredibly wonderful idea that it left me breathless—until I realized I'd be eating alone in my breakfast nook with Ming and the cats for company. Still, I couldn't begrudge Anna this opportunity or fault Wendy for her generosity.

"That's wonderful, Wendy."

Frances and Ariel voiced their agreement.

"The problem is, how do I get her to come with me and not get all upset because I'm paying for it?"

I considered this. Knowing Anna as I did, I knew what Wendy meant. The woman had her pride.

"How about thinking of something that you need her for? Like maybe—maybe you're still so shaky from the breakup that you need her there with you for a breakup buddy so you won't do anything stupid and jeopardize your job. I can't come with you because I'm working, or I would."

"Brilliant," Ariel said. "I've always said you should write screenplays."

"In the next life. How does that sound, Wendy?"

"Absolutely perfect. And guys? I've decided that when the sixty days are up, in the middle of March, I'm going to start dating. Nothing serious, I'm going to go out with a lot of men and have fun, and if someone special comes along, that's okay. But I'm going to take things very slow and be cautious before I get exclusive with anyone."

Now I really felt as if I was the slowpoke of the group. If even Wendy, who had been so emotionally destroyed by Rick, could think about dating again and decide to go for it, what was holding me back?

I decided to go for broke.

When it was my turn to have the floor, I stood up and said, "I could give you guys a cartload of bull about how busy the catering's been or how I've been trying to get my butt out there and socialize, but I'd be lying. The truth is, I've been at home most evenings with a good book."

Silence. Not a condemning silence, but a support-ive one.

"I'm not sure what's going on, but a part of me thinks that maybe I have some block against dating, maybe I really don't want a relationship in my life, and so that's the reason I'm having all this resistance to the process."

I knew all the right words. I'd read all those self-help books. I'd watched enough Dr. Phil, and even Oprah. So why couldn't I make it work?

Ariel, who almost always has an answer, was silent. Frances was looking at me, considering.

Finally, Wendy spoke.

"Do you want to get married, Eva?"

I had to be honest. "I'm not sure. Every time I've had the opportunity come up, I've run from it."

They all thought that over, then Wendy said, "What do you think of when you think of being married? What does it mean to you?"

"I'm not sure what you mean, exactly."

"When you see yourself married to a man, how does it feel in your daydream? What do you see yourself doing?"

It came to me in a flash, such a strong feeling that my knees literally gave way and I grabbed for a chair and sat down.

"Are you okay?" Ariel said, reaching my side.

"She's fine," Wendy said. "I think she just got in touch with something."

"Oh, shit," I said, burying my face in my hands.

"It's okay," Frances said. "You don't have to say anything until you're ready."

"Do you want some time?" Ariel said. "We could all go in the kitchen and bring out some more snacks."

I nodded my head. I heard footsteps fade, then slowly took my hands away from my face. Wendy was still there, sitting on the sofa to my right.

"I'm here for you, Eva," she said quietly. "The same way you've always been here for me."

There was a lovely quality to Wendy, and I knew she was going to make some lucky man a wonderful partner, and be an incredible mother. She went deep, every time, and wasn't afraid of feelings. As much as I loved Ariel, I thought this whole thing was a little too much for her. She needed action, and being stuck was something that made her uncomfortable.

"Were you abused?" Wendy said.

"It's not that. It's just—I think it's my father."

"In what way?"

"It was like—every time I tried to be who I was, to reach for what I wanted to be, he'd fight me."

"Give me an example." Wendy took my hand between her two and rubbed it gently.

I held on to that hand so tightly, like it was the only thing preventing me from sinking farther into a quagmire of emotion.

"When I wanted to go to culinary school, he thought it was a stupid idea. My mother helped me in secret, but she couldn't stand up to him. My great-aunt read him the riot act, then gave me the money to go. She'd never been married, and always lived her life exactly the way she wanted to, like Kate Hepburn."

"So you only saw the two extremes, a woman who had to minimize herself and hide important things in order to make her marriage work, and a woman who said to hell with it all and decided to go it alone."

"Yeah. That was it. I must know the wrong people, but I don't think I've ever seen a marriage where the woman didn't have to give up a lot more."

"While children are small, yes, I'd agree with you. They need their mother with them, and that's a fact of life no one can ignore. If you want to have children, the sacrifice is worth it. But it's totally different if you simply want a partner, Eva, a good husband. You shouldn't have to give up your life in a true partnership."

"Do you really believe that?" For one horrible moment I thought I was going to break down and cry.

"Yes, I do."

I looked into that beautiful face, those gorgeous clear blue eyes, and I marveled at her ability to still *believe* after the reality of stepping out of an eight-year affair with a supremely selfish man.

"The important thing is, Eva, do *you* believe it?"

"No."

Finally saying it was like a weight off my chest. But where did I go from here? If I didn't believe I had a future in a relationship, how could I have any hope of finding one?

"We'll work on this with you," Wendy said. "You're not alone."

Words I needed to hear. I leaned back in my chair and watched as Frances and Ariel came back into the living room, loaded down with every snack imaginable. Like good moms, they were going to feed me and sit with me and listen.

I was suddenly so grateful for them, for our group.

"Okay," I said when we were all seated around the coffee table, snacks in hand. "I don't think this is something that I can solve overnight, but just knowing about it might be enough."

"Why do you think I'm painting?" Frances said. "Sure, I want a show of my own, but I'm scared to death of another failure after my divorce."

But at least you were married once. At least you tried.

I didn't even have the energy to go for a sports or war metaphor, let alone a prison breakout.

"How about a journal?" Wendy said. "It really helped me."

"How about," I said, "I commit to writing an hour a day and try to get to the bottom of all this. Then at the next meeting, I can do a reality check with you guys."

"Works for me," Ariel said.

"Good idea, Eva," Frances said. "That's much more valuable than just forcing yourself to date."

"I think you'll find writing a great comfort," Wendy said. But the expression in those eyes told me that she regarded this discussion far from over.

CHAPTER 13

So off I went to Borders, but this time in search of a journal. I found one, a great spiral notebook, lined paper, with cats all over the cover, all sparkly and pink. Yeah, it was kind of girlie-girl, but I liked it. I purchased some fun pens in bright colors with ink to match at Staples and settled all of my new treasures at my workstation in my kitchen.

I set aside a separate drawer in my desk for all of it, and decided that, whatever was going on, I would write every single day from ten to eleven o'clock in the morning. The only exception was if I had a catering job, and then I had to make up the lost time in the evening.

Ten to eleven in the morning more often than not turned into ten o'clock to noon, but I wasn't counting. I wrote and wrote each day, as February ended and March began, feeling as if I was burning to get to the bottom of why I had such reluctance to pair up, to become part of a couple even though I told everyone that was what I really wanted.

But was it?

One good thing about a journal, you could be completely honest within its pages—no fooling around. And I made a promise to myself not to hide behind anything, even humor. If I was honest, this whole thing was just getting too painful.

Wendy and Anna did leave for Milan at the end of March. Wendy did a masterful job of convincing Anna that she needed her as a breakup buddy, that she still didn't feel strong. Anna had a passport, so that was no problem. The strange thing was, when it had expired, she'd automatically had it renewed. I think she'd always secretly hoped she'd have a reason to go back to Italy, and Wendy had provided her with one.

I begged Anna to find some new recipes for me while she was there, then loaded them both up in my van and drove them to LAX early one morning. Wendy insisted I merely drop them off at the curb. Since I knew she'd flown all over the world, and Anna wasn't an amateur world traveler, I let them out, helped get their bags out, hugged and kissed them goodbye and set off for home.

Ming looked despondent as I let myself in the door. He hadn't been fooled; he'd seen the suitcases. At least he hadn't peed on them, as Wendy's cat, Max, once had.

"Three weeks, buddy," I said, reaching down and

picking him up, cuddling him. "Three weeks for us to keep each other company and wait for them to come home."

Michelle's job kept her away as well, but it was good she was working because she needed the money. Still, it seemed strange to be rattling around in the house all by myself.

In a strange way, the solitude helped my thinking process. Yes, Ariel called and we went to a few movies, and Frances came over to make sure I wasn't too much of a hermit. We went shopping, and out for coffee. And I knew that, since our Hate to Date Club met every two weeks, we'd be having a meeting with just Frances, Ariel and me.

But life was good. Work was steady, even though April's usually not a booming month, so I was thankful for that. I had my fair share of husbands and boyfriends hit on me—what was it about a blonde with boobs in the kitchen, whipping up a few spicy dishes? And I came home from those jobs and found myself pulling out my journal and writing far into the evening about how I felt, seeing men basically betray their women, and their relationships.

Strangely enough, I began to understand that you could choose the way you looked at the world. It was the old "glass half-empty or half-full" thing—or half-assed, in my case. As Anna had once said to me, *You create your own happiness. You, and no one else.*

I couldn't keep blaming things in my life on the fact that I didn't have a man, a solid emotional partnership. I knew I had to do the work, and this journal was a part of that process.

With my experiences with my father, and some of the men in culinary school, I could have looked at men as just competitive assholes, roadblocks to any life that I wanted. But I didn't want to do that. I'd seen too many women friends of mine who, by the time they reached their forties, seemed old and hard and bitter. They became totally focused on their war stories about men—horrible divorces, immature boyfriends and idiot husbands.

They had their emotional blinders on when they stumbled across a good man, even a guy they could have been friends with. They were so locked into their weary worldview that no man stood a chance. Their glasses were definitely half-full.

I couldn't go there. Despite my father's lack of faith in the career path I'd chosen, I still loved him very much. I took no joy in the fact that I'd managed to make a success of a career he thought dicey at best. I'd never put a lot of stake in proving him wrong. What I meant by that is that I never felt the desire to rub it in his face. I knew that just by living my life the way I wanted to, I was letting my father recognize my values and what it was I wanted out of life.

Even if we were so different, we could still meet on the

common ground of family, and because we loved each other.

I also knew that if either of my brothers, or my sister, had decided to go for something outside his realm of what was safe, his reaction would have been the same.

So maybe, I wrote in my journal late one night, *it was all more about him than anything to do with me*. I smiled, then wrote, *Like this whole dating thing is more about me than about what's out there or what men I'm meeting*.

Things began to click. Early in the week, I got out my address book and called every single woman I knew and trusted. I told them all I wanted to meet a good man, and asked them if they knew anyone they could set me up with.

The classic blind date. Worse than any other kind of date I knew. But I was going in; I was taking that leap of faith straight off the side of that cliff. Like the fool in any Tarot deck, I was going to walk straight off that mountainside and see what I could see.

Or was that the bear?

Blind dates.
How do I hate thee?
Oh, let me count the ways...

The weird thing about blind dates was that they really showed you, as just about nothing else in life could, what your family and your friends really thought of you.

And this was't even addressing the fact that the guy was sizing you up. I had a male friend tell me once—after I had relentlessly pestered him—that men tended to quickly group women into recognizable groups, all based on animals. Fox, dog or cow. Fox meant a sexy woman, dog an ugly one, and cow, well, she had too much excess weight.

What was this with the animal symbolism?

As I sat at a table at Chandra's, a really terrific Thai restaurant on Arroyo Parkway in Pasadena, I studied the man who sat across from me.

I think you can subclassify men according to their externals. And it's always amazed me how closely you can guess their personalities from those externals.

Stan was of the subspecies *Teddy Bearis Comfortablis*. He was round and soft, with sincere brown button eyes and fluffy gingery-colored hair. He also had a distressing tendency to resemble the Pillsbury Doughboy. I didn't even want to think about what he might look like with his clothes off. Clothes that, I might add, looked like his mother had picked them out for him.

The sad thing was, he was a really nice guy. He just did nothing for me in the "sparks" department. That little click I talked about earlier.

But, on the plus side, I was out on a bona fide date,

and that was saying something. I could report back to our group that I had actually gotten out of my house and into the trenches. And the food was great.

"What do you think, Stan?" I said halfway through our appetizer. "I mean, I always get this little click when I know there's a possibility of a romantic relationship." *Romantic* was a softer word than *sexual*, though most men would probably prefer the latter. And everyone knew that a woman basically decided if the relationship was going to be sexual within twenty to fifty seconds after meeting the man.

"I—what do you think, Eva?"

I had a feeling he wasn't all that into me, either. This would make things easier.

"I think we have more of a buddy vibe."

He sighed and set down his fork. "Yeah, I think so, too. You know, I get that a lot."

For one moment I thought about giving him over to Michelle for a complete makeover, like that movie where this girl turned her best male friend from a schlub to a stud, then fell in love with him.

"I do, too," I said, and in a way it was true, even if I'd been the one making most of the decisions. "But I've been doing a lot of thinking about this—" I really had "—and I think it's all a numbers game. You told me that you worked as a computer programmer. Do you get out a lot?"

"Nope. My sister's friend set this up."

My friend, he meant. No matter, I'm not going to quibble.

"Don't you sometimes think this whole thing could be solved a lot faster if you met a lot more people?"

"Sure."

The beginnings of a beautiful brainstorm was starting up right at this table, among candlelight, the smell of exotic spices and a vase of orchid blooms.

"I'm thinking about hosting a huge barbecue sometime around the end of April, maybe early May, when the weather's really good, and getting together all the men I've dated who have become friends of mine. Would you like to be added to that list?"

"An all-male barbecue?" Stan said doubtfully. "Eva, how is this going to help me?"

"Oh, no, I'd invite every single girlfriend I had, so it'd be like a great big singles swap. *Huge.*"

Stan pondered this, his round, teddyish face creased into a frown, then said, "I like it. Put me on your list and count me in."

Talk about being proactive.

I went through my address book, my work contacts, my e-mail address list, everything. I even called Paige and asked her if she knew any single men in San

Marino. I made up a list of every bachelor I knew and drew up an invitation none of them had any hope of resisting—ribs, hamburgers, hot dogs, barbecue chicken and pork chops, and all the side dishes and desserts I could think of. I knew how to bait this particular hook.

Add in ice-cold beer, wine and some wild women, and we had ourselves a party.

I'd present this idea at our next Hate to Date meeting, and ask Ariel and Frances to add to the list of men and women. My house had a huge yard, complete with a barbecue area, so the number of people wouldn't be a problem. And in a funny kind of way, I was really hoping that Stan would find someone.

Heck, I was hoping I'd find someone.

I decided to include Stan in all the planning. He seemed nice but kind of lonely. And if Michelle made it home in time for the party—I was pretty sure she would—I was going to suggest an all-out makeover for Stan a few days before.

At the moment, I think he had my complete menu on a spreadsheet. And I'd also told him he could bring as many of his buds from work as he wanted to.

I decided to be the first one to speak at our next meeting in April. And I was jazzed—I had really gone all out.

"Remember how we said we'd just change our behavior and the feelings would follow? I said.

"Yeah," said Ariel. She and Frances were on alternate couches, facing each other but turned toward me. Ariel had the big calendar out.

"Well, the journal helped. In the last two weeks, I've been out on two dates, to a wine tasting, and I even endured a round of speed dating!"

To say that their jaws dropped would be an understatement.

"Eva, you really made a breakthrough," Frances said.

"Yep. And when I was out to dinner with this guy named Stan, who my friend Nancy set me up with, I had an incredible idea."

I told them about the barbecue at the end of the month, and they loved it.

"Can it be early May?" Ariel said. "That last weekend in April is horrible for me."

"You got it," I said. "How about Saturday the sixth?"

"What about Mother's Day?" Frances said.

"You're right," I replied. "How about the next Saturday, the thirteenth?"

"Perfect!" Ariel said, writing it into her Day-Timer.

We spent some time with Ariel and Frances listing their single guys and girlfriends, and then I ran off a bunch of invitations for them after changing the date to May.

We were well on our way.

When it was Frances's turn, she said, "Eva, you inspired me so much that I ran out and got a journal. The words are just pouring out! I can't believe how much fear I still have left over from my marriage."

"I believe it," I said. "I can't believe the stuff that's been coming out of me, just from the discipline of writing every day, same time, same place, basically same subject."

"That's it, I'm getting one, too," Ariel chimed in.

"It's *so* worth it," Frances said. "Here's my new goal, I made it up just as we were talking. I'm going to kick off my dating life at the big barbecue…my goal is to get my phone number to at least five guys. I'm really doing well with the painting, so I think I should have some sort of social life, too."

Ariel was next, and she surprised us.

"I think Nate may be the one," she said.

"He asked you out?" I said.

"We've been out a few times, to movies and things, lectures, but there was still this buddy-writer-screen-writing thing going on. I'd dress up like they were dates, with much more care than I usually did. Finally, we went out last weekend and he confronted me with the whole thing, asked me how I felt, what I wanted from our relationship, and he told me flat out what he wanted."

"No more just friends, huh?" said Frances.

"Nope. And I agreed. But I said I wanted to take it slow, and be free to date other men at the same time."

"Nothing like driving a man crazy, right?" I said.

"I want to make sure he's the one. But here's the crazy part. I think he is."

"Why do you think so?" said Frances.

"Because he's the only man who's ever really taken me seriously. I sensed it right away in the group. A couple of the guys would kind of brush aside my ideas, or say they weren't strong enough, meaning masculine enough. But Nate was always there, always fair, and always ready to offer comfort and support."

"That's priceless," I said. "Are you attracted to him?"

"Strangely enough, I am. When I started dressing up, he did the same. Out with the ratty clothing, the whole starving-screenwriter vibe, and in with the really nice, casual clothing. But if I had to say what the one thing about him was I liked the most, it would be his mind. And that hasn't changed at all."

"Good sense of humor?" Frances said.

"Great. No one makes me laugh as hard."

"How's he doing with the writing?" I said.

"He's come closer to selling something than I have. He works at one of the studios in Burbank, reads scripts and has friends in the industry. He's one of the hardest workers I know. I may be crazy, but I think he's going to make it."

"What about you?" said Frances.

"I'm not quitting!"

We talked far into the night, ordering in two pizzas. I made a salad, and I'd already made a killer dessert, a lemon pound cake with fresh berries and whipped cream. That, and coffee (and chocolate) rounded out the meal.

It felt fantastic to be back in the game.

A couple of nights later I was finishing up washing and putting away some of my own platters after a dinner party I'd catered, when the phone rang. I picked up, didn't recognize the area code, but decided to answer anyway. Who would be calling this late at night?

Michelle. Of course. Hawaii, with the unfamiliar area code.

"Eva? Did I wake you up?"

"Nope. I just got done with a job. What's up?" I poured myself a cup of coffee, doctored it up, grabbed a few pieces of chocolate and went into the living room, Ming at my heels.

"I—need some help."

Uh-oh. Right away, I knew it had to be something concerning John.

"Shoot. Wendy and Anna are in Italy, so I'm here alone and I have all the time you need."

"No job tomorrow?"

"Not for another two days. You've got me."

Silence, then, "Eva, I'm so damn stupid!"

"What do you mean?"

"I'm barely out of one relationship before I'm right back in another! How could I do something so stupid?"

"Slow down. Tell me what happened."

Frances had recommended one of her firm's best lawyers, and Michelle had gone to see her before she'd left for Hawaii. She'd wanted to start divorce proceedings, so Bryan would be left in no doubt as to what was going to happen between them.

"He called me on my cell—"

"Bryan?" I couldn't believe this. No, actually, I could.

"—and he told me the whole affair was a big mistake. Now, little twentysomething is getting all possessive and wanting him to make a commitment as soon as we're divorced."

This was too typically Bryan and, unfortunately, all too common. But this was also Michelle, and I wanted to be strong for her.

"You told him no, I hope?"

"Of *course* I did! I could never trust him again after what he did! So I told him that wasn't even a possibility, and the separation between us still stands."

Silence.

"So the problem is—"

"So the problem is, every other time I've worked with John, I've been married. Not single, not separated, but *married*. And I brought my wedding ring along, and wore it on the set—"

"He went after you anyway?" I didn't like the sound of this.

"No, no. It was just—I confided in one of the other makeup artists, she was going through a rough patch in her marriage and I told her I was in the beginning stages of getting a divorce. I forgot to tell her not to tell John and she did, and—"

"But why is that a problem? That he knows, I mean?"

"Because—because he asked me out to dinner, and he had this whole meal catered down at the beach at sunset, and—"

I was closing my eyes, imagining this, living vicariously—

"—and then he told me that he'd always been attracted to me from day one, and that if I was in the middle of getting out of a long-term relationship, he wanted to be first in line once it was over."

Wow. Tell me how you *really* feel, Mr. Dempsey. My instincts at the gallery opening had been dead on target.

In a world of men who "need time" or "my space" and "aren't quite sure of their feelings," who tell you, "it's really not *you*, it's *me*," here was a man who stepped up to the plate and put his feelings on the line. It sounded as if he'd had feelings for Michelle for a long time.

I thought it was all rather breathtaking.

"So I told John I wasn't sure and I didn't know if it was smart to think that way when I still had the divorce to get through."

"What did he say?"

"That life was too short and you had to reach for happiness when you saw it right in front of you."

I agreed with John Dempsey.

"And that—that he'd been waiting for a long time, hoping there might be some way we could be together, but not an affair. Eva, I'm scared to death that he's talking about the whole thing, marriage and everything, and I can't do that! What if he wants kids?"

"Does he?"

"Yeah." She sounded dangerously close to breaking down. I knew Michelle's history, and I knew exactly why she was getting emotional about this. She had good reasons.

"Okay. Can you tell him what happened to you?"

"Oh no, Eva, no! I can't tell anyone. You're the only one who knows the whole story."

"But Michelle, none of it was your fault."

"But it wrecked everything for me."

"That's your mother talking."

"I don't mean that way, I mean that I can't—I can't seem to have children. I think something happened to me back then. Look at how long Bryan and I tried, and nothing happened."

"But they have all sorts of things they can do now—" I stopped. "Okay. Forget your mother and forget Bryan. Forget the divorce, because you're legally separated now, and he was cheating on you, and you let the whole thing go and you've let him know you want to move on. So if you have feelings for John, don't go all guilty on me. You have *nothing* to be ashamed of. What I want to know is, if your mother and Bryan and all of the past had never existed, what would you want to do?"

Her silence told me everything.

"You really like this guy, don't you?"

I could hear her crying, even though she was trying to muffle it.

"Let it all out. You deserve it, you've been through hell."

So she did cry, and I understood. It had to be hell, having a breakdown thousands of miles away from any friends or loved ones, in the middle of a job where you simply had to be the consummate professional. She had to get it out now, with someone she trusted, and be ready for work in the morning.

I knew all about Michelle and the issues she had about trust. Much earlier in her life, a few of the people she should have been able to trust had let her down completely, in the worst way possible.

If I hadn't already figured it out in my journal, I was getting a front-row seat as to how the past colored the present. I was afraid that Michelle's past was going to make it impossible for her to have any sort of present, let alone a future.

But John Dempsey was a strong man, and I had this crazy feeling that he could be counted on. Trusted. He wasn't one bit like Bryan or Rick the prick.

"Do you want me to fly out there?" I'd do anything for Michelle. Like I said before, we'd met in the first grade, and had been friends forever.

"No, no, I don't want to disrupt your work."

"You come first."

"Thanks, Eva." She blew her nose. Her voice sounded tired.

"How's everything going with work?"

"Really great. It's a terrific script, and it's been cast really well. I like the director. All of the pieces are coming together."

"Are you just feeling guilty because technically you're still married to Bryan?"

"No, it's not that."

Wait a minute. My mind raced back through the conversation, then stuck on, *You're the only one who knows the whole story...*

"Did you ever tell Bryan what happened to you?"

Silence. Then, "No."

Now I knew what the problem was. John Dempsey wasn't Bryan, her ex. John struck me as the sort of man who would want true intimacy with a woman, no walls between them, no secrets. And it scared Michelle to death.

I took a deep breath and decided to chance it. What could she do, hang up on me?

"Are you scared to go after this thing with John because he's not Bryan? He's going to want to know all about you, and you don't want to tell anyone what happened."

"I can't, Eva. I can't. It still hurts too much."

That I could understand. But I had to keep trying.

"Look, I met John at that gallery opening, and call me crazy, but I think he'd understand. I think he'd give you all the time and the love you needed, and I think that if it turns out you really can't have children after what happened to you, I think he's the kind of guy who would love you enough to adopt. I think he's the real deal."

"I don't know, Eva. I—I'm scared. I like him so much,

I've never laughed so hard with a man or had such won-derful times. And that was even before he told me that he cared for me, before our dinner. I guess I'm scared be-cause—I can't just walk off this picture and I'm—I think I may do something that's not too smart."

"Have sex with him, you mean?" Personally, I thought that hitting the sheets with John Dempsey was one of the smartest things Michelle could do. Think of all the fantastic memories Michelle would have stored up for her old age even if things didn't work out! It's that old, you can really regret what you *don't* do sort of thing.

"Yeah. I feel like I've been fighting and fighting this thing between us. But now it's just—it's as if he's deter-mined that this time, nothing is going to get in the way."

Boy, did I love this man. Boy, did I envy Michelle. And boy, was I happy for her. But I had to think fast. I knew she was going to ask me for my opinion, and I had to be ready.

"Eva, what do you think I should do?"

"I think," I said carefully, "that you've had one of the toughest lives I've ever known. I think you deserve a little moment out of time, on a gorgeous tropical island, with a man who really gets you going. He's cared for you a long time, Michelle, and you should throw away your fears and sleep with him."

Silence. I could feel the pain she was going through.

"And I think you're good enough for him. I think that if he has you in his life, he's one of the luckiest men on the planet. And you know what else I think?"

"What?" she whispered.

"I think he feels the same way."

We were silent on the phone for a moment, then Michelle said, "Can I come and stay with you for a few more weeks after this shoot is over?"

"Sure."

"I mean, we'll still be finishing up at the studio, all the stuff on sets. But could I stay at your house until I get through this and figure out what's going on?"

"You bet."

We talked a little longer, then said our goodbyes and hung up. And as I set the portable phone down on the coffee table and reached over to pet Ming, snuggled by my side, I thought about what my friend was about to go through.

She was dealing with a man who was like a force of nature. He was sweeping into her life and forcing her to come alive again after a long, dormant sleep.

She'd been with Bryan because he was safe, but that safety had blown up in her face when he'd had his affair. The marriage hadn't worked for at least the last five years, so Michelle was way overdue for a love affair.

I got up from the sofa and started down the hall toward the library, Ming following me.

I sat down in one of the comfortable chairs and lifted Ming into my lap, then reached for one of the afghans and draped it over the two of us. Bongo and Riley were already asleep on my bed, waiting for Ming and I to join them. I'd stolen Anna's trick with the hot-water bottle, and it had done the trick with my feline friends.

Ming snuggled closer as I reached for the remote and turned on the TV. And there he was, in all his glory, John Dempsey in one of his first action-adventure roles. Cocky and swaggering, he filled the screen effortlessly in the way all the great actors do. I considered this little bit of synchronicity a good omen.

"Welcome to the family, you sexy beast," I said softly. "You'd better have your head on straight when it comes to my friend, or I'll be having a few words with you."

But I knew my words were idle threats. I just hoped Michelle could see him for who he truly was.

CHAPTER 14

Michelle knew that she could call my cell phone anytime, day or night. I just had to let it go and say a little prayer that she would find it within herself to see the good man who was standing right in front of her.

A really great man, considering it was John Dempsey. Okay, so I was seduced by his movie-star good looks and incredible charisma—but he was a good guy. My intuition was screaming that to me. I had no idea how the whole thing was going to turn out, and couldn't have predicted how complicated it would all become.

As for my love life, something had snapped inside me. I'd finally gotten it. The I Hate to Date Club had worked its magic, I was now a fearless serial dater. I responded to every blind date, every social engagement. I walked up to groups at cocktail parties and joined in the conversation in a way I wouldn't have even a few weeks ago.

I saw the whole thing from a different perspective. It was merely a matter of getting out there, and the right man would come along sooner or later. Like Woody

Allen was once supposed to have said about success, "Ninety percent of it is just showing up." It was the same for dating. For life, really.

I could barely face even thinking about being single for the rest of my life, to be honest. You can be stellar at your career, have excellent friends and family, wonderful animals, a great home, even take fantastic vacations each year. But the thought of endlessly navigating those years by yourself for the rest of your life is one of my greatest fears.

I'd done the Thanksgivings and Christmases when I'd come in the door all bright and cheery, and after a certain interval, maybe while drinks were being served, maybe at dinner, facing the unpleasant realization that I was the only person not in a relationship, that somehow I'd become the token single person.

I always had to scrounge up a date for a wedding. If something went wrong and I had to go to the hospital, I called a friend. I slept alone at night, and worried about the future, when it would be so comforting to be able to lie in someone's arms and not feel so terribly alone.

I knew that not all marriages had that level of intimacy, and that a lot of married women felt alone. But I also knew that there were a lot of marriages out there that did work, and those women were fortunate.

Yes, I knew all the stuff about a woman needed to be complete in and of herself. I agreed. Still, life was a lot more pleasant when you had someone in your corner who loved and adored you, and you felt the same way about him.

I had, at various times in my life, been described as a cockeyed optimist, or a hopeless romantic. But what was the alternative? The bitter brigade of women in their forties and fifties? By their sixties, a lot of them had simply given up.

So I threw myself into dating with a vengeance. I was going out two and three times a week!

And during that time I didn't meet one man who lit that little "spark."

Frances and I arranged to meet at the Bodhi Tree in West Hollywood for an evening seminar on soul mates. Yes, I know, Dr. Phil has said they don't exist, or that you shouldn't hold out for one. But the whole concept was so damn enticing, so Frances and I decided to go. Besides, there might be some cute guys there.

Ariel wasn't into it, she had a date with Nate. Then she came up with the idea of dragging him to the seminar so we could check him out.

"I really, really think he's the one," she said to me

over the phone the morning of our evening seminar. "But I want you guys to give me your opinion."

"Sure," I said, glad that one of us was that much closer to being part of a couple.

I loved the Bodhi Tree Bookstore. From the shelves of fascinating books, to everything smelling of incense, the candles, the statues, the wind chimes, the pictures on the walls, even the resident cat who wandered around, one of the most mellow animals I have ever seen.

They even brewed herbal tea for their customers.

The seminar was in the annex, a huge room just next to the actual bookstore on Melrose Avenue. Frances and I got there early and saved two seats for Ariel and Nate.

"What if we hate him?" Frances whispered to me as she kept her eye on the door.

"What matters is what Ariel thinks of him," I said. The whole Bodhi Tree thing always put me in a mellow mood. Give me a couple of metaphysical books and a great cup of coffee from the Urth Café just down the street, and I'm cool.

We both saw them enter at the same time, and I liked the way they looked with each other. The way they were with each other. Again, I was going with externals.

I would bet money Nate was from the East Coast, likely New York. There's just something about New York men. I really loved them. They had an attitude and a confidence that I found really attractive.

He was wearing jeans and a wonderful sweater, a navy blue cabled thing that looked warm—and nice shoes. A great jacket. I liked the way he was with Ariel, protective and watchful without being overbearing about it.

She was just glowing.

"Hey, guys!" she called, and started toward us.

"I like him," Frances whispered.

"Yep," I said.

The lecture was so-so. None of us bought the book. But what I liked best was the break, when Frances and I got to talk with Nate. I really saw what Ariel meant. He was smart, but not the kind of smart that makes other people uncomfortable or condescends. He was just a smart, funny man, and with his dark hair and eyes, no strain on mine.

I got this feeling, looking at both him and Ariel. And I had a very strong feeling that Ariel would find herself exclusively dating Nate before long. He was a keeper, and it was clear he was mad about her.

They didn't join us for coffee later, and as Frances and I sat outside at the Urth Café and had our coffee, we discussed them.

"She's staying over at his place tonight," Frances said, adding another packet of sugar to her latte.

"For the first time?"

"Yep. Her publishing house just put out this really neat astrology book, and the author was nice enough to do her and Nate's chart, and to give her some dates that would be great for their first time together."

"You can do that?" I said. It made sense. With a divorce rate that was slightly over fifty percent, you needed every little advantage you could create for yourself.

"I guess so. But my guess is that they're going to be just fine. What do you think?"

I took a sip of my latte, set it down. "I think he's the one. They both looked so happy with each other, they had that little glow."

"Yeah," Frances said softly. Then she perked up. "Hey, the first success of the I Hate to Date Club! We've all been out there doing our best, and Ariel actually found herself a keeper."

"It gives me hope for the future," I said. "One of us did good."

I catered a baby shower later in the week, and of course couldn't help thinking about Michelle. If anyone should be a mother, it was my childhood friend. She'd never had much family to speak of, and had always wanted one of her own. I could've kicked Bryan, her ex, for being so selfish.

I kept the menu simple, foods that were easy to eat buffet style. But the cake was the showstopper. It was darling, it looked like the cutest little stack of baby blocks. A rich chocolate (at the mom-to-be's request), I iced the different-size blocks with pastel shades of buttercream and added letters on the sides. I leaned toward blues, because the prospective grandmother had told me her daughter was having a boy.

This was a more traditional shower, not the couples showers that recently had become all the rage. This was definitely a total estrogenfest, and a joyous occasion.

As I packed up everything and prepared to go home, I wondered what it would be like to have your life in order like that. To know that you were beginning your family. It had to be a wonderful feeling.

Michelle came home in April, and the moment I saw her I knew something was different. It worried me, because I had naively thought that if a woman slept with John Dempsey, she'd look like she was lit up inside, as if angels were singing. Michelle just looked beat, and I didn't ask any questions.

When we got home, she just carried her bags up the stairs and crashed in her room, facedown on her bed. I let her be. I'd known her long enough to realize she'd come to me with any of it when she was ready.

The house was starting to fill up again. Wendy and Anna would be back from Italy in another week, and I was sure they'd have wonderful tales to tell us. Anna's birthday was at the end of April, so I began to plan the cake and food for a small, informal party at the house.

Work still occupied a lot of hours, and I was still out there dating, but I worried about Michelle. She looked tired and drawn even after she'd slept, and I sensed there was some sort of battle going on within her. She'd phoned her lawyer immediately upon coming home, and more wheels were set in motion.

There was nothing I could do unless she asked me. She didn't look as if she was in emotional danger, or depressed. Just navigating some rocky feelings.

In the meantime, I had a barbecue to plan.

I threw a little impromptu bash when Wendy and Anna came home. Ming was absolutely ecstatic, jumping all over the place and whimpering until Anna picked him up and hugged him. Even the cats seemed pleased.

Wendy and Anna brought home all sorts of gifts from Rome and Florence, Venice and Milan. And Anna brought home those promised recipes, carefully written down in a small notebook. I was in heaven as I fooled around with ways to use them in my business. I'd make them all at home before I tried them out on my clients. Once I knew they worked, they would go in my master recipe file in my computer.

I was happy to have the house full again, the company at mealtimes. Michelle had eaten with me, but a lot of the time I'd sensed she was far away, and I hadn't wanted to push her. She had a lot to think about concerning her future and what it was she wanted.

I began to plan that barbecue like a general planning a military campaign. RSVPs had been pouring in; a lot of people wanted to come. It made me feel better about the whole thing. One thing I knew about parties, the huge ones were a lot easier than the intimate dinner parties, at least I believed so. I loved a big crowd, lots of food, good music. How could you go wrong?

Stan and I were on the phone almost every other day, planning. He was really getting into the whole thing, and I think he'd invited about half his office, which was fine by me. It was my experience that men like Stan and his office mates made wonderful partners—if you could find that "spark."

Anna took over the garden, weeding and planting and even mowing the lawn. She used my little push mower, and I have to admit the grass looked better than when I'd hired one of the guys down the street with his huge riding lawn mower.

We cleaned the patio area and all the lawn furniture. I checked to make sure the barbecue was in perfect condition and ready to go. And Stan and I started making our huge shopping list. He'd insisted on going in on some of the food with me, and he was so into it that I agreed.

We stocked the bar, bought all the nonperishables. We decided to decorate with Chinese lanterns, they'd look so pretty when the sun went down. He even asked me to make a small batch of my barbecue sauce so he could taste it before the party.

We had a kind of trial run when we celebrated Anna's birthday on April twenty-seventh. I planned the party out on the patio, and the lanterns were all up and glowing. I'd ordered in a huge meal of Chinese food from the Golden Panda, but baked the birthday cake myself. Ariel and Frances joined us, and I invited Stan and a friend of his, Bob.

They both looked like typical computer geeks. I saw Michelle studying them during dinner and told her my idea about giving them both makeovers before the barbecue.

"Sure," she said, but I could see circles beneath her blue eyes.

"I could help," I offered.

"Eva, you're doing too much with this extravaganza already. It won't take me long to set the two of them straight. Do you think they'd be offended if I took them shopping?"

I had already broached the subject with Stan and knew the answer would be no. I told Michelle as much.

"Then let's set up a date before the party so they have time to get used to their new clothing."

I'd asked Michelle if she wanted to invite John and she'd said no. In a way, I understood. This was a barely disguised singles' scene, a meat market, and if John Dempsey was perceived as being on the market, we'd risk some sort of riot. Not to mention the paparazzi that might decide to fly overhead in their helicopters.

The morning of the party, the thirteenth of May, was bright and clear, and I was relieved. I wasn't really worried about rain, I could've probably fit everyone inside the house, spilling over from the living room into the kitchen, hallway and library. But it was so much more convenient to have everyone outside.

Anna was in charge of Ming, and I'd shut Bongo and Riley upstairs in my bedroom. I didn't want Bongo terrifying any of my guests by grabbing a rib or drumstick off their plates. I knew what he was capable of, and I'd set aside some chicken to give to the cats later.

I'd started cooking a couple of days ago, especially the sauce. But I'd done the majority of it this morning. Huge bowls of potato salad and coleslaw sat in my walk-in refrigerator, along with chicken parts, ribs, steaks, hamburger meat and hot dogs, all ready for the grill.

Stan and Bob had come early and I'd been stunned by their transformations. They'd really thrown themselves into it. Michelle truly was a genius, because they no longer looked like nerds. They looked like really nice guys who knew how to dress and carry themselves.

Stan offered to man the barbecue, and I decided to let him, as it would give him something to do. He looked like a very happy teddy bear, and a rather prosperous one at that.

"They look great," I murmured to Michelle as I poured ice over the bottles of beer and cans of soda in huge tubs to the side of the buffet tables.

"They were *so* cute," she said, heaving another bag of ice my way. "And so open to anything I wanted to try. I actually tweezed their brows and cut their hair."

"A vast improvement," I said, sitting back on my heels, satisfied that all the drinks were now iced. "We'll get those two paired off if it kills us."

"The sad thing is, they're really nice men, but the way

they were dressed would have turned off so many potential dates."

"You are the supreme master," I said.

She laughed, and I was glad to see her feeling happy.

The barbecue was a smashing success. It was fair to say that a good time was had by all. The food received raves, and I actually got some business out of it once some of the women discovered I was a caterer.

Stan's makeover had given him a ton of confidence, and he was the star of the grill, serving up people and cracking jokes. I noticed several women hanging around the barbecue area. Bob hung with his buddy, helping serve drinks.

I circulated, and walked up to any of the men who caught my eye. There were quite a few. I managed to have almost eight men take down my number before the end of the evening. The fact that they'd figured out I was the cook helped a lot.

Ariel arrived with Nate, and the two of them looked like such a *couple*. Wendy talked with him, and I could tell she liked him a lot, as did Michelle. And Anna gave me a very subtle look of approval, so I knew Nate had passed her test.

Frances circulated as madly as I did, I could see her shining hair through the crowd, flitting from group to group. By the end of the evening, she was sitting at one of the tables I'd put out in the yard and talking with a really nice guy, a veterinarian who worked in Alta Dena.

It came in handy, this catering job. I knew where to rent tables and chairs, cloths and plates and flatware, all sorts of things. The sun had set a while ago, the lanterns had blazed to life, and Anna and Ming had retired for the night. The backyard truly looked magical, and if I'd been catering this party for someone else, I would've pronounced it a complete success.

Stan came up to tell me he was leaving and surprised me by enveloping me in a—no pun intended—bear hug.

"Any potential dates?" I whispered.

"*Seven* women talked to me! I couldn't believe it! I got their phone numbers and I'm just going to date around for a while and make up for lost time."

"How did Bob do?"

"Three phone numbers! His mind was totally blown, he usually walks out of parties like this with nothing, nada, zip. Me, too. I want to thank Michelle, she did so much for us. It was more than the clothes and stuff, she really built up our self-confidence."

"I'm so glad for you both."

"Eva, there are a bunch of guys at the office who are

going to want to ask for her help when they hear about this. How much do you think she'd charge?"

I could see a nice little career developing for my friend on the side, one that would dovetail nicely with her professional makeup career.

"I'll make sure to ask her and I'll call you, Stan. Did you see where she went off to?"

"I think she went into the house a while ago. Do you want me to help with any more of the cleanup?"

"You and Bob have done enough. Go on home and bask in your accomplishments."

He smiled down at me. "I can't thank you enough, Eva. Did you meet anyone?"

"A few possibilities."

"This was a fantastic idea. We should make it an annual tradition. We could have it at my house next year."

I was up for the challenge, though I hoped I'd find someone before another year passed. "Sounds great."

I walked Stan to the door, said goodbye, then headed back outside to continue what little remained of the cleanup. Ariel and Nate had already left, as had Frances. Wendy was walking around, picking up empty plates and glasses and putting the disposable stuff in the large trash can I'd set outside while taking the rest into the kitchen.

When she saw me, she came up to my side.

"Eva? Michelle doesn't look too good. I saw her heading upstairs. You might want to check on her."

"Okay. Can you handle the rest of the cleanup?"

"Sure. I've talked some of the guys into helping me."

It was comical, really, the way they almost drooled over her. And even sweeter was the way Wendy was kind of oblivious to it.

I went inside and upstairs, to the bathroom that Michelle and I shared between the two bedrooms. I wondered if she was coming down with a summer cold or something. She hadn't looked good since she'd come home from Hawaii, and I wondered if she'd been pushing herself too hard. That was the way it was in her line of work. You didn't work for months at a time and then, *boom*, you were working nonstop. Feast or famine.

All that work, plus the pressure on her from her fears about a relationship with John—she'd probably reached a point of nervous exhaustion. A couple of days of sleeping in and some good comfort food would set her right.

Outside the bathroom door, I could hear Michelle vomiting.

"Micki? You okay?"

"No."

"Anything I can do?"

After a short pause she opened the door and I saw

utter devastation on that familiar face. She looked as if she was beat, and knew it.

"Oh, Eva," she said quietly, and her mouth trembled. "I think I'm pregnant."

CHAPTER 15

I'd been so used to Michelle *not* being pregnant all those years she'd been trying to conceive with Bryan that I was so stunned I couldn't speak. Then I realized whose baby she was carrying and I found my throat closed even further.

This couldn't be happening. My friend had been the object of derision and scorn, of painfully cruel gossip in our small Midwest town when she'd found herself pregnant at seventeen. Now the future mother of a superstar's child, this would be far worse. The possible humiliation could be on a global scale.

I didn't know what to say. I found that all my faith in John Dempsey and what a wonderful man I thought he was seemed like nothing in the face of something like this.

"Does he know?"

She shook her head.

"Are you going to tell him?"

"I don't know."

I hesitated, then said, "I think you're going to have to."

"Right. And then I can hear the old brush-off, the heave-ho, all over again, just like the last time!"

She wasn't thinking rationally, she was back in the past with Carl, her high-school boyfriend who had abandoned her at her most vulnerable time, but not before asking her, "Whose is it?" And with her mother, Margie, a religious fanatic who had tried to "beat the devil" out of her.

Michelle had walked to my house that February night without her coat, barefoot, in the middle of a snowstorm. Her mother had let her out of the house with barely any protective clothing, but not before beating her black and blue. She'd gone berserk when she'd discovered her only daughter was unmarried and pregnant. A sin like that had to be punished, there was no other way.

Michelle told me years later that she'd thought that night her mother wasn't going to stop until she killed her. When she'd loosened her painful grip on her arm for just an instant, Michelle had darted out the front door into the snow.

My mother had taken one look at her and hustled her upstairs into a warm bath. I will never, for as long as I live, forget the way Michelle had shook as she'd held on to the railing and tried to climb our stairs to the main bathroom. My father had finally had to carry her upstairs.

I wondered, years later, if her mother had hoped she would lose the baby that night, would lose what she regarded as a source of shame and sin. It was beyond comprehension, the way that woman's mind had worked.

Michelle had moved in with us that night and never returned home. She'd tried to continue high school, but small towns can be cruel, and she ended up dropping out.

Four months into her pregnancy, she'd lost her baby. It had been her and that baby against the world, against Carl and her mother and most of the town. When she'd lost her baby, she almost lost her mind.

She'd never spoken to her mother again. She'd gotten a job at the factory across the railroad tracks and moved into a small studio apartment. And she'd started a long, painful, downhill slide into the life she thought she deserved. If the entire town thought she was nothing but a whore, if her own mother believed it, then what had it mattered what she did?

I'd gone away to college, then to Italy, always feeling as if she should have been with me. When I came back home I'd tracked Michelle down at a party.

She'd been stoned and drunk, scantily clad, propped up in a corner, one of the equally wasted guys looking at her with casual interest. And I'd known, at that exact moment, that if I headed out for California and my dream and left my best friend behind, she'd be dead within five years.

She had that self-destructive urge within her, it had been planted there from the time she was a child. She'd been told she was nothing, told she was sinful and evil for so long that she'd started to believe it. When we'd seen the movie *Pretty Woman* together, I'd totally understood that line when Vivian said, "Why is it so much easier to believe the bad things?"

I knew that what we both needed was a brand-new life, so that night at that party I'd told her this big lie about how I couldn't make it to the West Coast without her, that I needed her to come with me. If she didn't, I'd never get my dream.

I'd brought her back home that night, and my mother and I had cleaned her up, fed her, loved her back to life. When we left two weeks later, my mother cried as she hugged Michelle, thanking her for making this trip with me so that I wouldn't feel so alone in an unfamiliar city, among strangers.

Then I'd gone to culinary school and she'd discovered she had a talent for makeup and took some classes.

We'd both started getting work in our chosen fields, she'd met and married Bryan, and the rest, as they say, was history.

I knew she remembered that baby, because she'd lost it in April, and always thought of it at the same time every year. We never talked about it, it was still painful to her. And I could've kicked myself, because I'd forgotten the date this year. I'd picked her up at LAX on that day, the same day, so many years ago, that she'd lost her baby.

My father had driven her to the hospital and my mother had never left her side as the doctor examined her. They'd brought her back home and told no one, but of course one of the nurses had known who she was and had spread the word. My mother would've had an actual fight with Michelle's mother if she'd dared come around our house.

But she hadn't. She had just gone to her church and told the entire congregation that her daughter had fallen into sin and couldn't be saved.

After the death of her child, Michelle had reminded me of a little alley cat, the kind that didn't trust anyone to be kind. It was always in her eyes. She'd had enough of human cruelty to last a lifetime. We'd talked far into the night as we'd driven out West, about how both of us wanted to start our lives over. But for my friend, coming to a city where no one knew her past had been a blessing.

Now I couldn't figure out what to do, how to protect her.

"There's nothing you can do, Eva," Michelle said wearily. "It's kind of ironic, isn't it? Here I thought things might be different, and it's all coming out the same. But this time—" her eyes filled "—I'm going to keep my baby no matter what anyone says."

"Of course you are." I had to get her to bed.

I walked her to her bedroom, helped her undress and get into bed. She asked me to set up a bag in case she was sick again, and I did, doubling two brown-paper market bags and placing them right by the head of her bed.

"Don't tell anyone, Eva, please. Don't let anyone know."

"I promise."

But as I walked out of the bedroom and closed the door quietly behind me, I didn't know if I could keep that promise.

I had coffee with Anna in the morning, but didn't say a word about Michelle. Yet she knew something was wrong.

"Is Michelle sick?"

"A summer cold, I think. She's been working too hard."

"I'll make her some of my chicken soup."

"That would be perfect." I noticed the small stack of handwritten cards by her coffee cup. "You haven't opened all your birthday cards."

"Some of them aren't birthday cards."

"What do you mean?"

Anna smiled gently. "When you get to be my age, receiving a handwritten note takes on a whole new meaning."

I understood instantly. It probably meant that a friend of yours had passed away and someone else was writing the note. I couldn't even begin to imagine what that was like, to slowly lose all your contemporaries.

"What do you do, then, if you don't open them?"

"I open them, Eva. I just need to wait for a day when I feel strong. Then I open them all at once. It works better for me that way."

"I see." Another plan was formulating in my brain. I had to do something to help Michelle, but I couldn't betray my promise. I had to figure out what was going on with John, and if there was any hope for the two of them. If the way he'd looked at her during that gallery opening was any clue, I thought they had a chance.

"Anna, would you look after Michelle for me today?

Give her some soup and see that she sleeps? I have a catering job I have to get done."

"Of course."

I drove out to Malibu, where I'd heard John had a home. I didn't drive out without a plan. I'd taken a look at Michelle's cell phone, and found his home number. I dialed while sitting in my van, in one of the parking lots overlooking the Pacific. I just hoped he was at home this Sunday.

He was, and remembered me instantly. In fact, he was so sharp that it was hard for me to kind of talk around the issue.

"Is she okay?" he said. "She's not returning my calls."

I had to see his face. I had to do this for Michelle, to protect her. But I couldn't have this discussion over the phone.

"Could we meet somewhere for coffee?" I said. "We have to talk."

We met at a Starbucks along the Pacific Coast Highway. Malibu was a funny little town, where movie stars, musicians, actors and politicians could sort of lead a normal life because so many of them were located in such a small area.

Not too many heads turned when John walked in,

dressed in well-worn jeans and a T-shirt. Well, a few female heads turned, but not because he was a star. The man just had it.

He'd barely sat down at my table with his coffee when I blurted out, "What are your intentions toward my friend?" I felt like a Jewish mother to the max, but I had no choice.

He smiled, and it reached those eyes, and suddenly I knew everything was going to be all right. My insides stopped shaking.

"I'm going to marry her," he said quietly.

"Good." I hesitated, then blurted out, "Do you want kids?" In for a penny, in for a pound, I always say. Open foot and insert mouth.

"Kids with Michelle, yeah."

I melted inside. I wanted to cry. Finally, *finally*, good things were going to happen for my best friend. But I had this terrible feeling she was going to fight them every step of the way.

"You must be wondering why I'm meddling," I began.

"You love her and you're worried about her."

When I stared at him, openmouthed, he said, "She's told me all about you and your family, the fun times you had in high school, the way you both drove out to the West Coast."

"Did she tell you about her mother?"

He frowned, then said, "She told me her mother and father died when she was a baby and your family adopted her."

Oh, Micki…

I sat back in my chair, wondering what to do.

"Let's go back to my house," John said suddenly. "We can whip up some lunch and have a long talk."

"Yeah," I said, still flying blind.

If someone had told me I was going to go to John Dempsey's house and have lunch with him, I would have laughed my head off. Yet here I was, in a Mediterranean-style kitchen, a glorious working space, with every gadget known to humankind. I should have been in hog heaven, but I was too worried.

"I can't make lunch," I said, and meant it. I was frozen, in shock. I still couldn't quite believe Michelle was pregnant.

"We'll order in."

Over pizza and beer, out on his deck right on the ocean, we talked.

"There's some stuff about Michelle you have to know, in order to love her the way she deserves to be loved," I said, taking a swig of my beer.

"Shoot," he said, reaching for another slice.

I don't know what he thought I was going to say, but

he never finished that slice. I'd decided to go for broke because a part of me knew that my friend wasn't going to risk her heart again. In fact, I'd had the strongest suspicion that she was planning on finishing up this film and pulling a disappearing act until her child was born.

It was that alley-cat thing. She wasn't going to allow anyone to hurt her, ever again.

I told him everything, even about the pregnancy. Maybe I was wrong to do so, but I didn't think so. If he loved her the way she needed to be loved, it would all work out for the best, no matter what I said. But he couldn't go in ignorant, or Michelle would just turn him away. He had to know what he was up against.

"If this makes a difference to you, what she's been through, what she's done, if it makes you love her less, then I want you to walk away now and don't give her any false hope," I said quietly. I couldn't believe I was saying all this to this man, this whole afternoon had been surreal.

He sat looking out at the ocean for almost a minute before he answered.

"That's why she's not talking to me."

"Yeah." I leaned back in my deck chair, totally exhausted.

"Can I drive back to your house with you? To see her?"

I have never, ever, in my entire life, been so glad that my instincts about a person were correct.

"Sure."

"Will you stay in the house so if things get rough I have someone on my side?"

I had to laugh at that. This, from a man who blew up bridges and detonated bombs? Of course, that was movies and this was life. "She's going to kill me when she realizes what I've done."

"I'm not going to tell her that you told me anything. I'm going to say that I saw you here today in Malibu, driving home from a catering gig, and I flagged you down and asked you if she was okay. I thought something was wrong because she wasn't returning my calls. And then you suggested I come on over and see for myself."

"That'll be enough to get me in big trouble."

"Ah, not that much. We can handle it."

I liked that *we*. "You should consider writing scripts, your stories are that good. I think this just might work." Then to my complete surprise, I put my face in my hands and started to weep. It had all been too much, remembering. Like Michelle, I'd put that part of our past deep in the past, not wanting to remember such a painful time.

It had hurt so much, seeing her go through all of it

and feeling so damn helpless. Even with my mother and father helping, and with me right beside her, she'd seemed so alone.

"It's okay," John said, and I felt a warm hand squeeze my shoulder. "She can't resist the two of us."

That's true. I mopped myself up after taking the handkerchief he offered.

"You're one pretty terrific guy," I said just before we headed out for Pasadena, and home. "You don't have any single friends, do you?"

We drove back to my house, and I went upstairs to tell Michelle she had company. When she came downstairs and saw John standing in the living room, her accusing gaze turned to me.

"Eva, what have you—"

"Nothing," I said, remembering the plan. "I saw John in Malibu while I was driving home from a catering job and he flagged me down. He's been worried about you, you haven't been returning his calls and he didn't know where you lived. He asked if he could catch a ride back here with me, and I thought it would be okay."

She looked as if she wanted to kill me, but we'd had worse fights before and survived.

It must have been the pregnancy, because she started

to cry and John was across that room so fast and had her in his arms in record time.

"I'm going to go make a pot of coffee," I said to no one in particular. Tea, coffee, whatever. They both work in an emergency.

I made that pot of coffee and cut myself a slice of cheesecake from yesterday's barbecue. Since I didn't hear any yelling or the sounds of things being thrown and broken coming from the living room, I suspected everything was going all right.

I walked to the kitchen window above the sink that overlooked the backyard and saw Anna sitting at one of the tables on the large patio. Ming was in her lap, and she was slowly opening her stack of envelopes.

I hoped some of them contained good news.

Life was so strange—the news of a death in one envelope, a new life beginning for my best friend. It all kept turning round and round, and as Anna said, "You have to store up the good times in order to face the bad. You have to make your own happiness, choose to be happy."

She was right.

I had no idea where I was going or what would happen with my life. I only knew that I was happy for Michelle and I loved having Anna and Wendy stay with me. Ariel and Frances were good friends, for life. I would take things day by day. But no matter what happened, I knew I'd be okay, and I knew I'd survive.

I knew I'd be happy.

Wendy walked into the kitchen. She looked kind of shaken.

"I thought I was having a hallucination," she began.

"John Dempsey *is* in our living room," I said quietly.

"Really." She smiled. "Tell me what's going on."

"He's in love with Michelle and wants to marry her."

Wendy couldn't stop her smile from turning into a grin. "That's right, they were working on that movie together. Does she love him?"

"Madly."

"Then I'm glad." She poured herself a cup of coffee and joined me at the window. Glancing out, she saw Anna.

"I think she had a good time in Italy with me."

"I know she did."

"I saw him," she said quietly.

It took me a heartbeat to realize she was talking about Rick, her married man.

"Where?"

"At a party in Milan. He had to have been following me, after finding out where I was working."

"What did he want?" But I already knew.

"He wanted me back."

I hoped she hadn't given in.

"What did you do?" I was almost holding my breath.

"I said no. And meant it."

I let my breath out. "I'm so proud of you."

"I could never have done it without you and Anna. I can't even begin to tell you both what you mean to me."

"I know. Right back at you." I glanced out the window again. "Let's take Anna a cup of coffee." I'd made decaf, thinking she might like some.

As we walked outside, Anna glanced up and began to gather her envelopes together into a neat pile.

"Nothing too bad, I hope," I said.

"Two old friends are gone. The rest were birthday cards."

"I'm sorry."

"Thank you, Eva."

I went back in and got the cheesecake, and we were cutting pieces when John and Michelle finally came outside. Her eyes were all red and puffy, but she was smiling. He looked tired but happy.

"Hey!" said Wendy. "You're looking a lot better, Michelle."

"I feel a lot better," she said, and she and John joined us at the table. I went back inside and got more plates, forks, spoons, cups and saucers, more cream and sugar. Like always I was serving food, a lot of the time at turning points in people's lives.

Today was no exception.

Michelle was making introductions as I came back out, and John had that relaxed way about him that made me feel as if he'd been with us for a lot longer than just this afternoon.

"So," said Anna, getting straight to the point. "What news do the two of you have for us? Michelle, you look like you're about to burst with it."

"We're getting married," Michelle said. "Eva, I want you to be maid of honor, and cater the whole thing, and bake our wedding cake."

"Sure," I said, reaching for another piece of cheesecake. I glanced over at Anna and she smiled, and I could feel so clearly what she was trying to convey to me.

This is happiness, these moments. Store them up, treasure them. Keep them close, to warm you when life isn't kind. But choose happiness, Eva, because it's a far better life when you do.

"So," I said, addressing John, "is she going to let you have any say in this whole shindig?"

"I doubt it," he said, then laughed.

I already felt like he was part of the family. Wow.

"And about those friends of mine, Eva?" he said.

"Yes?" I said, really, *really* liking the sound of this.

"I'll make sure every single one of them is invited. I'll even personally introduce you."

"I'm going to hold you to that promise," I said, then, "Wait right here."

I always keep champagne on ice because I'm always looking for an excuse to open it. It's that old glass-half-full thing again. I went inside and got a chilled bottle and five flutes, then raced back outside.

"A toast!" I said, setting down the flutes and then expertly opening the champagne. There are perks to my job, and knowing how to properly open a bottle of champagne is one of them.

I filled all the glasses and we raised them up high.

"A toast," I said, "to both of you. May you always love each other as much, or even more, than you do now." I gave Michelle a quick glance. "And a toast to any children you may have, now or in the future. To the family you're going to create."

"To family," Anna and Wendy echoed.

"In any form that it takes," Michelle whispered, tears in her eyes.

"To good friends," John said, looking at me pointedly.

Now I really got why legions of women went to every single one of his movies. Those *eyes*. Michelle was one lucky woman.

"To good friends," I said. "To *best* friends, both old and new. And to having the courage to start a new life when you find the right person. Congratulations, both of you," I said, right before we all drank the sparkling wine there in my backyard, with the sun shining down on all of us.

Our cup wasn't just half full, it was overflowing.

In late August and on a gorgeous summer day in Malibu, Michelle married John.

All of us got together and did what we did best. I saw to the food, and baked a spectacular wedding cake.

Ariel helped me set up all the catering details, and it wasn't so bad considering there were less than one hundred guests. She also did all the flowers and kept the master list—complete with different colored pens—to make sure that everything got done in a timely manner.

Frances helped Michelle with the invitations, making the whole thing look like a big blow-out barbecue that would turn into a wedding once all the people John and Michelle loved best in the world were at his house in Malibu.

Wendy and Anna helped Michelle pick out a stunning dress, a designer original, and Wendy managed to get Michelle a great deal on it with all her connections in the world of fashion. And she helped Michelle do her own makeup and hair right before the big event. Anna was there to hold her hand and play surrogate mother all the way.

Of course, I bawled like a baby through my water-proof mascara, even though I was maid of honor, with Wendy, Frances and Ariel all backing me up as brides-maids. And Anna was there, in one of the front pews reserved for family, with such a smile on her face.

We actually pulled it off, because as the reception started, none of us heard any helicopters overhead, or any other indications that any of the paparazzi had gotten wind of the fact that one of the biggest stars on the planet had just gotten married.

They looked stunning together, but more than that, they looked *right*. Michelle was glowing, so happy with her pregnancy.

All in all, a great time was had by all, and was going to continue far into the night.

So there we were, the four of us, sitting around one of the round tables just off the dance floor that had been created inside the huge tent next to John's home. I could see Anna two tables over, in an animated dis-cussion with a *very* handsome older man, and I wondered if her life would have yet another act. I'd keep her as a roommate as long as she wanted to stay, but a woman as vibrant and full of life as Anna? My bet was that she'd be on to the next chapter of her life before long.

So I sat with Ariel on my right, Wendy on my left, and Frances next to Ariel. There were twelve seats per table, but we had this one to ourselves.

"Isn't it ironic," Ariel said, pushing away her finished plate of wedding cake, "that Michelle was the one who said she was never getting married again, and yet here she is, the one who made the leap."

"Thank God for John's money and lawyers," Frances added. "I was glad to see Bryan get out of the way."

"Imagine when he turns on the news and finds out!" Wendy said.

"To true love," I said, raising my flute of champagne.

We all raised our glasses and drank.

"That was a wonderful toast you made, Eva," Frances said. "Straight from the heart."

"She's my sister in every way that matters," I said, and the several glasses of very expensive and very good champagne I'd consumed made me a little sentimental. "You all are. You've seen me through some pretty tough times."

"Did it work?" Frances said. "I mean, the whole Hate to Date thing."

"Well," said Ariel, ticking everyone off on her perfectly manicured fingers, "Nate and I finally got together," she said, and we all glanced over to where Nate was talking with a group of men John had introduced him to, very in-fluential men who could get a screenplay sold and produced.

"Go on," Wendy said.

"You got out from under the relationship you were in," Ariel said. "And with looks like yours and a posse like us, you'll find the right guy."

"The strange thing is, I know I will." Wendy's expression was both content and animated. She'd changed so much from that first discussion at Starbucks last January, she seemed much more sure of what she wanted and how to go about getting it.

"Frances is dating her veterinarian, and I have a good feeling about this man," Ariel said. "Are you guys exclusive yet?"

"Yep. Both of us have dated around enough to know gold when we find it."

"Excellent!" said Ariel. "So you see, that leaves—"

"Me," I said, brought down to earth with the prover-bial thud. "But I'm on my way, too—less coffee, choco-late and solitary nights with books. More getting out there, asking questions, going to parties. You guys have to admit, I've been trying. And I think that it's turned out *so* well for all of us, we don't really need meetings every other Sunday. We could do one dinner a month and just play catch up. What do you all think?"

I was blabbing and I knew it. But I was absolutely determined to put on a good front. This was Michelle's wedding, after all, and I didn't want anything to compromise this moment. Weddings were for happiness, not for depressed introspection.

I'd have *plenty* of time for that when I got home tonight, got into bed and pulled the covers over my head. I might even give in to that irrational panic that there was no one out there for me, that even *Anna* had less trouble finding a man. That it would be me, my cats and my cooking for the rest of my natural life, hating to date all the way to the grave—

"Is Eva at this table?" said a masculine voice.

We all turned en masse, then gaped.

Luke McConahey, in the flesh. Another actor who, if you don't know who he is, you've been living in a cave. Just over six feet, dark hair, blue eyes, a body to die for and bone structure that makes the camera love him.

He blasted into the public eye playing Nick Fox, a cynical smuggler with a heart of gold in a science fiction series on cable that achieved cult status. There was no one who'd ever made packing heat sexier. Then he made the leap to feature films, and had starred in several movies with John Dempsey, playing his world-weary but devastatingly sexy sidekick.

If there was a bridge that John Dempsey couldn't

blow up, Luke would find a way. A cynical, wisecracking kind of buddy, he had testosterone to burn and then some.

"Eva?" he said again, but he was looking right at me, a grin tugging at his lips and total masculine anticipation in those eyes.

"That would be me," I said. My heart was already speeding up and I hoped I wasn't blushing. Could it be that easy? *We met at a wedding . . .*

"John told me I'd find you at this table," he said.

I nodded. "And you have."

He grinned, full out. I melted. "Want to dance?" he said.

He held out his hand and I took it. Warm, firm, just right. Better and better. Total silence from the table now behind me as I walked out on to the dance floor and he swung me into his arms. I felt like the bubbles in my champagne flute.

Oh my God, I was going to dance with Nick Fox, space pirate, and bad boy extraordinaire. Life didn't get any better than this.

As if my life had suddenly turned into a perfect old movie, the band started into a slow, romantic song and we fit together as if we'd been dancing all our lives.

So I'm getting ahead of myself right about now, anticipating the future. So, who wouldn't? My feet are barely touching the ground, I like this man a lot, but I still have to figure out who he really is beneath the parts he plays. The one thing I do know is that if he's a friend of John's, he's probably a good guy—and certainly no strain on the eyes.

But there's one more thing I know. However this chance meeting turns out, whatever happens, I'm going to be fine. I won't be hiding under the bedcovers or behind a book with a latte at my side. I'll be out there, looking for love, until I find it.

I want it all. Like Anna says, I'm choosing happiness.

"John tells me that you cook," Luke says.

I glance up at him. Neither of us can stop smiling.

Yep. Whatever happens, I'll be just fine.

Hearing that her husband
had owned a cottage in England
was a surprise. But the truly
shocking news was what
she would find there.

Determined to discover more about the cottage
her deceased husband left her, Marjorie Maitland
travels to England to visit the property—and
ends up uncovering secrets from the past that
might just be the key to her future.

The English Wife

by Doreen Roberts

Available June 2006
TheNextNovel.com

HN47

They were twin sisters with nothing in common…

Until they teamed up on a cross-country
adventure to find their younger sibling.
And ended up figuring out that, despite
buried secrets and wrong turns, all roads
lead back to family.

Sisters

by Nancy Robards Thompson

Life is full of hope.

Facing a family crisis, Melinda and her husband are forced to look at their lives and end up learning what is really important.

Falling Out of Bed

by

Mary Schramski

HARLEQUIN

Nxt

HN41
Available May 2006
TheNextNovel.com

There comes a time in every woman's life when she needs more.

Sometimes finding what you want means leaving everything you love. Big-hearted, warm and funny, Flying Lessons is a story of love and courage as Beth Holt Martin sets out to change her life and her marriage, for better or for worse.

Flying Lessons

by

Peggy Webb

Available May 2006
TheNextNovel.com

REQUEST YOUR FREE BOOKS!

2 FREE NOVELS TO INTRODUCE YOU TO OUR BRAND-NEW LINE!

There's the life you planned. And there's what comes next.

YES! Please send me 2 FREE Harlequin® NEXT™ novels and my FREE mystery gift. After receiving them, if I don't wish to receive any more books, I can return the shipping statement marked "cancel." If I don't cancel, I will receive 3 brand-new novels every month and be billed just $3.99 per book in the U.S., or $4.74 per book in Canada, plus 25¢ shipping and handling per book plus applicable taxes, if any*. That's a savings of over 20% off the cover price! I understand that accepting the 2 free books and gift places me under no obligation to buy any books. I can always return a shipment and cancel at any time. Even if I never buy another book from Harlequin, the two free books and gift are mine to keep forever.

156 HDN D74G 356 HDN D74S

Name	(PLEASE PRINT)	
Address		Apt. #
City	State/Prov.	Zip/Postal Code

Signature (if under 18, a parent or guardian must sign)

Order online at www.TryNEXTNovels.com

Or mail to the Harlequin Reader Service®:

IN U.S.A.	IN CANADA
3010 Walden Ave.	P.O. Box 609
P.O. Box 1867	Fort Erie, Ontario
Buffalo, NY 14240-1867	L2A 5X3

Not valid to current Harlequin NEXT subscribers.

Want to try two free books from another line?
Call 1-800-873-8635 or visit www.morefreebooks.com

* Terms and prices subject to change without notice. NY residents add applicable sales tax. Canadian residents will be charged applicable provincial taxes and GST. This offer is limited to one order per household. All orders subject to approval. Credit or debit balances in a customer's account(s) may be offset by any other outstanding balance owed by or to the customer.

NEXT05

She had no choice but to grow up fast.

A woman reflects on her coming-of-age
in this dramatic tale of a daughter torn
between the love of her life and
the family that needs her.

The Unspoken Years

by
Lynne Hugo

Available May 2006
TheNextNovel.com

Is reality better than fantasy?

When her son leaves for college, Lauren realizes it is time to start a new life for herself. After a series of hilarious wrong turns, she lands a job decorating department-store windows. Is the "perfect" world she creates in the windows possible to find in real life? Ready or not, it's time to find out!

Window Dressing

by Nikki Rivers

Available June 2006
TheNextNovel.com

HN48